This book is dedicated

Dearest Mike,
Thanks for buying
+ one day maybe
reading! :)
love ya,
Michele
11/2018

Prelude

Who doesn't love fall?

My favorite time of year. Even in hotter-than-hell East Texas. Little known fact about Texas: It takes 24 hours to drive from the northern to southern point and 24 hours to drive from east to west. 24 hours. Good grief. That's why I picked this place. I am "dead," but no one would find me if they even thought otherwise.

I'm on my daily late afternoon walk with the dogs, listening to Pink's *U + Ur Hand* on my headphones ...*I was fine before you walked into my life...*

My favorite part of my day. The temperature dropped and is holding at 80 versus the normal 90+ in October. Must be result of all the hurricanes, or global warming. Who cares; I'll take it. Big live and red oak trees cover the streets, forming a majestic archway for those to follow. Shades of green, yellow, red and gold pop out all over. The builders put in curved sidewalks to give it a more serene setting for this private affluent community. How nice of them.

I listen to music on the lowest setting, always on alert, one earpiece out. I wave at the few neighbors with a friendly smile, but rarely engage in conversation, using the pretense that I'm talking on the phone. I left everyone, there's no one for me to call. The neighbors think I moved here after my husband's death and that it's a family lot that I inherited. East Texas money. Either oil or farming. My direct neighbor owns land to farm watermelons. Must supply the whole state, as he's not hurting. Four homes and this one is the smallest at 7,000 square feet on 10 perfectly manicured acres. Fucking watermelons. Who knew? Must keep that in mind for my next life.

My dogs, Bruiser and Koda, are German shepherds and they walk obediently beside me. They appear friendly, but trust me, they take badass to the next level. They are gorgeous and I selected them from an elite K9 military training facility. They were gifted to me for all that I did. I deserve a lot more. The dogs are my only family right now. They are gentle and fierce, graceful and deadly. They are committed and determined. They only need to know 3 commands. Play. Alert. Attack. They are precision. I could probably have them shit in the bag if I wanted to, but I put on the appearance that they are your normal everyday playful puppies when we stroll through the 'hood. People see what they want to see. Fools. God, I love these dogs. (Why do people have chihuahuas or dachshunds? Really, any dog under 25 pounds is just a damn rat.)

Every day for 12 months, I have done the same thing— waiting, watching, observing and listening. After what I will call "FUBAR," I spent the first 6 months recovering in a military hospital in Germany, or Hell Spa Landstuhl, as I called it. My head, liver and spleen were lacerated. A hundred stitches in the head. All my ribs on my left side broken, lung collapsed, both rotator cuffs torn, road rash on whole left side from where I was dragged, broken femur, broken wrist, chin obliterated. I may be leaving some things out. I really don't recall the first two months.

I had my own private doctors and nurses attend to me. This was a dream assignment for them. They wouldn't have to work again after this rehab stint, as they were paid enough to never return. They weren't given a choice on that, either. They wouldn't be returning. Period. They took this rebuilding to the next level. Think bionic women times 10. I was deceptively strong at 5'7. Slender frame, long legs. Strong enough to choke grown men begging for mercy. Let God have mercy on them; that was not my job. The new titanium implants ensured I could use other body parts to do it now, too. Not only did they mend the broken body parts, but they transformed my physical looks, too. I was always a looker, but hell, I must admit, I was damn near model-looking perfect after they were done. New teeth (oh yeah, some of those were gone again after FUBAR), new nose and chin line, 34 full C breasts lifted. Bonus. Hell, yeah. My hair color was now a crisp deep auburn versus dirty blonde, which made my blue eyes pop even more. I have a dark blue rim around my irises, with flakes of yellow and translucent blue in the middle. They are mesmerizing and penetrating. I had worn brown contacts before, so was able to go back to my true color. Thank God for that, those contacts were a pain. IPL on any freckles and my skin was a glistening and flawless Cherokee tan. I was unrecognizable from before, and utterly drop dead gorgeous, if I do say so myself. What a waste, too, since I was alone; utterly alone.

Twelve months. Lots can happen in a year. You don't even notice. I didn't think I'd ever get out of Landstuhl, but I did. I rarely sleep, and luckily have the pooches take turns with me, so I can. Each day, I follow a simple routine that I mix up so it's never the same. I do hard cardio with an online Peleton class, and try not to kick everyone's ass, including the male man-tight-wearing instructors pedaling to a remix of *Come Sail Away* (who knew the remix would be so good). When they start on a 25 resistance, I'm on

60. Take that, skinny bitches. I change my online profile constantly to keep anonymity while allowing me to feel included during my self-inflicted exclusion. I do another hour of hot yoga to stretch out what still needs to mend, and then 90 minutes of Kenpo, a martial art combat sport that combines multiple martial arts to finish off opponents with strikes and kicks. This isn't any Kung Fu Panda crap. My online instructor is amazed at how I started at a white belt and moved up so quickly. If only he knew I was a certified double black, before. I should be an actress in my next life...or selling watermelons.

After spending grueling hours on my body each day to ensure it is in top form, I walk the dogs and then actually spend more time in my secluded backyard on drills with them to keep them sharp. When I'm not giving myself a break with a little music, I'm listening to all the latest intelligence reports that I've hacked into. My custom Patek Phillippe watch gives me alerts, making an Apple watch look like a Timex from Walmart while giving me a female version of a James Bond prototype. That was a gift I got myself. I deserve it. I'm worth it.

And on this glorious fall day with a little wind blowing, the sun shining, the cool crisp of autumn in the air, and my head tilting to the sky to absorb all the sunshine...for a moment, I *almost* let go of my senses. George Winston's *Thanksgiving* is playing, a bit of a change in pace from Pink. Hypnotic, soothing, and relaxing, while inspiring. A sixth sense had me look down the street at the car coming towards me—a car I'd never seen before in this town. This small town is littered with Mercedes, Range Rovers, BMWs, and Bentleys, so when a yellow tricked-out taxi cab came rolling through, I knew it was not picking someone up to take to private airport. F' me. I needed just a little more time. The bait was taken quicker than I'd expected. I leaned down to Bruiser and Koda and took off their leashes while whispering into their ears. Just like that, they were gone.

I selected this little sleepy community so I could have time to rest and prepare. Alanis Morisette's *You Oughta Know* shuffles on, taking serene to anger just in time...*And I'm here to remind you... It's not fair to deny me...*

To quote Kurt Russell from *Tombstone*:

 "You tell 'em I'm coming...and hell's coming with me, you hear? Hell's coming with me!!"

Chapter 1
The 'rents

My life started in Montgomery, Mississippi, or at least I thought it did. Population was a big whopping 8,700 at the time. My parents are Jeff and Kelli Leonard. They weren't my real parents, but the people who adopted and raised me. Mom and Dad were devout Catholics and conceived 5 times, each ending in a stillbirth. They decided to go the adoption route for number 6. That's where I come in. They wanted a boy. They got a girl. They named me Matti. Yep, with an "i." Wanted me to be special all my life and never have a necklace or key chain that would spell my name the same. I'm thinking they still wanted a boy, with that name and the fact that my room was blue until I was 13.

Dad was the high school coach, athletic director, history teacher, and occasional custodian at the only high school. When you only have 128 students, you pretty much must do a little of everything. Mom was a stay-at-home mom who volunteered at the school for every event (a requirement when you are married to the AD), and she volunteered at the church.

Montgomery's demographics were right down the line, basically 50% white and 50% black. You might have a few Hispanics or Asians thrown in, but pretty much just black and white. No pun intended. Mississippi is surrounded by Tennessee, Alabama, Louisiana, Arkansas, and a small coast of the Gulf of Mexico. If you don't know your geography, go get a damn map.

Lots of mixed marriages in Mississippi. Not my parents—
they were as white as white can be. Dad was 5'9"—said
he was 5'10" but we knew better. He was stout, with
blonde hair and blue eyes. He looked like a coach. Short
trimmed hair and tan lines from being outside all the time
wearing short sleeves and socks. (I can only imagine what
Mom thought when he came to bed with those tan lines.
Oy. Maybe that's why they turned off the lights. Just
saying). Dad was good-looking and a good man. He cared
for the kids and literally would give them the shirt off his
back. He backed his co-workers and basically ran the
school. Many of the white families sent their kids to the
only other private school in the city, meaning that most of
the students were African-American. It doesn't take an
astrophysicist to do the math, here. There were 8700
people in town, 128 students at public high school, and
another 75 at the private school, meaning not a lot of
higher education going on, here. Dad was determined to
make a difference and change that. Dad had a master's in
education from Rice University. Do the math on that one.
Why anyone would get a master's in education from a
prestigious university only to make $40K/year was just
plain crazy. Dad returned to live in Mississippi where he
grew up. I always felt like he was settling. He told me he
was determined and felt it was his calling. Something
didn't add up, though.

Mom looked exactly the same as Dad, being blonde and
blue-eyed, but she was 5'2" and petite; a petite little
perfect china doll. She was a cheerleader in her day and
was quite the looker. What was most impressive was,
good God, did she have a pair of lungs on her. You could
hear her yelling down the field: "Get open!" Everyone
suspected that Momma Leonard was the true play caller

for the teams. She was highly respected in the community as being someone who would tell you how it was and not hold back, but in a way that was not divisive or demeaning. She knew her shit and did not tolerate others who didn't. You would have thought she had an extra 12 inches on her. Mom attended Austin Peay University in Clarksville, Tennessee. She "said" she had a degree in physical therapy, but to be honest, I didn't feel like that could be confirmed, but couldn't figure out why she would lie about it.

Mom and Dad LOVED me. Imagine that you lost 5 children. Bet your ass you are going to coddle that next one. I could do no wrong and no one ever suspected I was adopted, as I looked just like them, too. Hell, I didn't even figure it out till later. Dad being a coach, I trained with him each day. When you live in a 1A school district, you naturally get "selected" for every team. I played volleyball, soccer, basketball, ran track, and then even performed on the drill team. Outside of school sports, I swam and did gymnastics. I called some of these activities "character building." Like track. They put me on hurdles. Sick fucks. Not hitting my full height potential until later in my high school years, I was with 7 other girls and placed last every time. I was the only white girl on hurdles. I learned to laugh when I finished what seemed like minutes after everyone else. Took a bow, too. I was the only kid who begged to run the 2400. Know why? Only 6 people in total ran in the 2400 in an open race. Boys and girls. I dusted them every time. Hallelujah. Took a bow on that, too. How's that for character?

I got free "coaching" from Dad, but Mom was the one who was my sidekick. She didn't do "let's cry, eat donuts and watch *Beaches"* to get over things. More like, "What the hell are you whining about?! Are you going to settle for that? Let me answer for you, NO. Now, try it again." I always thought she was secretly training me for something. Just wasn't sure for what, at the time. Failure wasn't an option with her; she told me repeatedly that I was made for something special. Wasn't just that Catholic religious talk squawking: she knew it in her core.

Although I naturally excelled in pretty much all athletics, my education didn't start out as smoothly. When I started kindergarten, my teacher called my parents in to say she thought I might have "special needs." Mind you, this was *kindergarten* in a state ranked 45th for education. Holy shit. WTF?! Mom and Dad didn't believe it and called in a tutor from Montgomery, ALABAMA – which was roughly a five-hour drive. Only a few states behind Mississippi in education and you got it, Ala-fucking-bama was one of them...so I'm not sure what they were thinking with that selection.

Miss Peterson tuned out to be a godsend: a little overweight, early thirties, African-American teacher who was soft spoken and kind as kind can be. She did a 6-hour assessment on me. SIX hours might have well been an entire lifetime, at that age. She started by giving me a white piece of paper with 24 squares on it. She told me to draw in one box. I drew something in the last box. She then told me to draw in another, so I drew in the one right beside it and worked my way back to one by the time I was done. She looked at it and smiled. At age 5, I had drawn the 24 hours in a day and had been exact in the setting of the moon and sun. Miss Peterson looked at my Mom and Dad and I'll never forget what she said. "Oh, she's special, alright; she is very special indeed. Most people can finish a story if you start it; this special little lady can tell you how it began based on how it ended." She didn't say it like Viola Davis said in *The Help*, "You'se be special," but you get my point. I took it that I was similar to Robert Downey Jr. in *Sherlock Holmes*. Miss Peterson moved to Montgomery, Mississippi from Montgomery, Alabama that weekend, and from then on out, I was tutored after school by her in the spectrum of gifted and talented. Turned out Miss Peterson was significantly gifted, too.

There was no getting around this. Most people waited all their lives to figure out what their skill set was. Mine came early, for me. Seems "special" here had a photographic memory which led me to master statistical analysis and computation, which tied into time and process management. By 8, I slept less than 5 hours a day. I read everything in sight. I was damn near like John Travolta in *Phenomenon*, a walking encyclopedia; or Scarlett Johansson in *Lucy*. It was trying for me to converse with other people as, well, let's face it, they were fucking idiots. I wish I could be like them just occasionally, but it wasn't in my DNA, which led me to compute much earlier that I wasn't Jeff and Kelli's kid.

At the age of ten, I asked my parents who my real parents were. This would be an eye-opening conversation. They hemmed and hawed at first, and asked why I was bringing this up. I remember thinking, (1) I look like you in features, but not like you (2) You brought some chick to tutor me from Ala-(fucking)-bama on a coach's pay from Mississippi, and (3) Mom has me on a regiment that would make Navy Seals look soft, so I'm just thinking that maybe something more is up. Want to tell me the truth now, or keep up this charade?

I remember it vividly. Mom and Dad looked at each other, hesitant and defeated. "Just tell me the truth, I'll figure it out soon enough." I wasn't fully expecting what they told me.

Mom looked at Dad, whose shoulders had sunk, and said, "Let's cut to the chase. Your mother attended FBI Academy and was a Special Agent in Charge for the Department of Treasury. She was on a mission; you were brought to us when she died during delivery."

(WTF?!) "Ok, wait a minute. I think you may have left out a few important points. Let's start from the beginning."

She closed her tear-misted eyes, one small trail running down her face, and then slowly began to tell the full story. Dad held onto her hand with his eyes closed as she spoke. She told me my biological mother had always been driven by something, even at an early age. Her loyalty to this country was never questioned. Mom smirked when she explained my real mom was expelled from school once for beating up a boy who was trash talking the President, and then told me about the time that the principal threatened to give her "licks" after she misbehaved in class and she said, "You might want to think twice about that. My mother has never touched me; you can bet your life she's not going to allow you."

Mom told me story after story of how my birth mom was brought up, how she applied to the Academy in Quantico, how she excelled in all aspects, and how our government immediately knew the asset that they had in her. They didn't know much after that, as her missions were top secret and little information was disseminated, but she communicated via different channels whenever she could, for their safety. They didn't even know she was pregnant or was dating or married to any man, but one fateful day in July, they were contacted by a stranger who brought me to them and told them my mother had died in childbirth. There was a note she had written before she passed, and it said simply, "I'm sorry. Go to the well."

Umm, ok. "Where and what was in the well?"

Mom laughed. "You are your mother, there's no doubt about that." She continued to explain that they went to retrieve whatever was in the well in Alexandria, Virginia in a backyard of an old house. There was a briefcase with instructions, different currency, a locked case which had vials, and a key to a lockbox. Mom told me to hold on a second while she walked back to the office and came back with an envelope and handed it to me. I looked at it with calculation (versus in trepidation). I slowly took it out and opened it. The note simply said, "If you are reading this, something went seriously wrong. We talked about this and what you need to do, but I left out an important detail. Take care of my baby. Trust only Freddy. I love you."

Mom stopped for a second and said, "I'm sure this is confusing, so what do you want me to explain first?"

I looked at her for a long second. My shoulders lowered as I focused on controlling my breathing before I said, matter-of-factly, "So, you must be my aunt, and Dad therefore is my uncle. Alexandria is where you grew up. Freddy is either someone she met at the Academy or worked for, and who brought me to you. We can get to the vials and instructions in a sec. I guess the only question I have right now is: "What was her name?"

Mom and Dad looked at me, incredulous. They had just told a 10-year-old about her mother's death and my only reaction was to know her name. Mom looked at me and simply said, "Patti; her name was Patti."

"How did she spell it?"

"She spelled it P-a-t-t-i."

Well, at least it explained my fascination with names ending in "i" bullshit.

I walked over to Mom and Dad, lowered my head, and hugged them. They were both crying uncontrollably at this point. Not me. I did have a profound realization that these people who were in fact relatives who didn't choose this situation, were doing all of this for me. I had an immense respect and gratification towards them and loved them not because I had to, but because they deserved it.

I was late for practice and told them I had to go. I looked back and forth to each of them and said, "You are the only mom and dad I'd ever want or will ever have." With that, I got up and walked out the front door.

Mom could be heard wailing from down the street.

Chapter 2
Bust a Move

Quick calculations. Assuming he/she/they didn't see me yet, the yellow taxi was traveling at 30mph and roughly .9 miles down the street. They'd have to stop at the 4-way stop sign so not to give notice to others and would have to turn left and drive another half a mile to get where I was going. A few other cars were on the road, so that might slow them down a bit. Now, if they did see me, I was fucked, but I was placing good odds that (1) they couldn't afford to do a drive-by first, as cameras litter the streets, (2) they must be fucking stupid to pick a yellow taxi versus any other non-descript Uber-type vehicle to fit in, and (3) most importantly, they hadn't started speeding up yet.

Regardless, I had just under a mile to get back to my property by cutting through the common area of our neighborhood. My house was on a 5-acre lot and the first in our private little community entrance. I selected this house for the easy access to get out, but knew I could potentially risk unwanted visitors. Our houses surrounded a man-made lake, with their acreage in the back of the houses versus the front. Many had large privacy fences of brick or stone at front of their entrances, while mine didn't, since I was the first house, with a dense common area beside me. I had a long driveway entrance, as my house was nestled more towards the middle of the property line with an infinity pool and a pond behind me before you hit the dock for the lake.

My fastest mile run pre-injuries was 4.32, just 20 seconds off world record. Time to figure out how rehab was working. I toggled on my headset to the next song to get me going. *Awesome God* came on. Crap, not that one right now. Toggled again. *Bring Me to Life* by Evanescence. Oh yeah, this ramped up and had a pounding chorus, perfect for what I needed...*Wake me up inside...Save me from the nothing I've become...*

I took off towards the house.

My house was a one-story architectural find. God, I hoped it wasn't about to be shot to hell, after this. It had beautiful stonework that covered the outside, with gas lanterns all around. It was U-shaped, with the front portion of the house a big great room with the kitchen, dining, and family room all together with large open windows that looked out to the back's incredible views. On one side of the U there were the bedrooms with the master at the end, while the other side had a large media and game room and a garage designed with a car collector in mind with storage for up to 8 vehicles. Every room was ginormous, in true Texas fashion. Every side to the house opened to the center. Outside, in the center of the U, was the sparkling blue infinity pool with cascading falls, a diving board, and a swim-up bar that ran the length of 25 yards. Trees were scattered all over the manicured lawn, with leaves starting to fall. The pond was about half an acre away with benches and fire pits surrounding it to sit and relax on, or you could use the bridge for quicker access to the other side. The dog run was on the side where I'd trained Bruiser and Koda. Past the pond, if you followed the crushed granite trail, it took you to the dock where a modified Boston Whaler 230 and two Ultra 310X Kawasaki jet skis were fueled and ready to take off on the lake our houses surrounded.

Inside, the ceilings were vaulted with cedar beams, with a hacienda ranch décor of pure-white walls with brown cedar accents. Not overly decorated, but they would be considered pristine and refined. The white and gray shale marble countertops in the kitchen were offset by steel Viking appliances with two farm sinks, two ovens and two refrigerators, and two 150-bottle wine fridges. Two large white layered brick fireplaces adorned each side of the great room, which made it perfect for entertaining (if I had any guests). Large vintage rugs in red, blue and gray gave it a pop of color but tied it all in. I really could get used to this place. The spacious master was complete with sitting nook and another fireplace with an ornate wood mantle. Two shower places, two closets, two powder rooms, were all tied together with a massive iron chandelier. Too bad there was only one person to use all this.

Everyone in the neighborhood had updated security. I had no idea why, but we seemed to attract retired athletes or State Farm and Sabre execs to live here. Plus, we had 'ol watermelon farmer dude beside me. I guess some were afraid that someone would steal one of their championship rings or their wine collection. I had state-of-the-art military-level security, installed since I had mine tied into theirs so I could see anything that they could from my house. Better than a drone. More like the setup that Christian Bale (Hot) had in *The Dark Knight*, where he used everyone's cell phone to triangulate the Joker. Inside in one of the makeshift bedrooms I had a hidden sitting room concealing an arsenal of weapons. You name it, I had it. Wall beds came in handy for concealing the large, spacious suite. My artillery was like Keanu Reeves's (also very Hot) underground weapon room in *John Wick*. I had no less than 12 handguns, my favorite Colt Python, a few submachine guns, shotguns, rifles (the DTA Stealth Recon Scout is a beast), and few more goodies to round it out, like my badass safe.

The only way to get close enough to my house was to come straight down the driveway or through the back lake. What were they planning? Maybe they'd try to go to a neighbor's? Pretend like they stalled on the road and need help? Come barreling down the driveway with automatics blasting? Depended on who was at the wheel. I'd made a few enemies over the years; some domestic and some international, with only a handful that would agree to this mission, once contacted.

Think. Yellow taxi. What was the significance of that? That ruled out domestic. No one trained was that stupid. Well, maybe, but the odds were diminished. Must be international. Visions of FUBAR flashed through my head. I winced just thinking of the physical pain I'd endured. I could will myself to endure it again, but they got one shot, so they better hope it counted.

I was grateful for the 80-degree weather today. I felt karma was on my side. It made the last 200 yards to get on my property go even faster. Just 200 yards to door. I could sense in the back of my head that they'd turned at the stop sign, so they must be at a point where they turned down my driveway or not. Tick, tock. How many were in the car? That made all the difference in what I did next. I could make it inside, but I'd have my back to them and would be an easier target. If it was just one, then I knew my next move. Tick, tock. Taylor's Swift's *Look What You Made Me Do* shuffled on ...*No, I Don't like You...*

I was going with only one. I felt inspired today.

I stood in my driveway with an elevated pulse rate, but barely breaking a sweat. I'd been training for this all my life. I stared at the driver's side which was now coming full speed down the driveway. *Tell me who it is. Show me your God. Damn. Face.*

3

2

1

Motherfucker.

I can't believe it's him. He's alone. Rage must have taken over his already-dimwitted senses, as clearly, he was an idiot to come here. This validated what I was working on. I looked down at my left foot and remembered what had happened last time. I'd told him I would fuck him up the next time I saw him.

Miguel Badham was his name. Kind of looked like the actor John Cusack. 6'2", black slicked-back hair, strong chin, brown, beady, messed-up eyes. I swore he was like Harvey Keitel in that he showed up at every GD situation. He was a damn cockroach and truly pure evil. Evil is not racist; it's not biased; it's just evil to the core. You could not reason with a crazy person and you could not reason with evil, either. I could see the sides of his mouth curving up in a knowing smile.

He braked within inches of hitting me. He wouldn't run me over. I didn't flinch. He'd want to take his time. He was a contract hit man, kind of like me. The last time I saw him, I was in Positano, Italy. What should have been a beautiful vacation getaway turned into a 12-hour torture fest hosted by this sick fuck. Waterboarding was the least of my concerns, and when that ended up unsuccessful, he decided to go full Kathy Bates, in *Misery,* on me. I was tied up from head to toe on a super yacht off the coast and he took a mallet to my left foot to start the fun. (Why did everything happen on my left side? Not that I was going to be a foot model anyways, but it took a team of doctors to fix what he did. I affectionately called my pinky toe 'snaggle,' as the tendon couldn't be lengthened anymore and it occasionally got hooked on the other toes. Fucker. You couldn't tell, if I was in heels or flats; just when I took it out of shoes and tried to point my toes. No ballerina shoes for me.)

You couldn't hear my muffled screams and whimpers, as the boat was anchored far enough away from others and the crisp, blue, cloudless sky filled with sunbathers and cruisers, skiers and tourists, all enjoying the sights and sounds of the positively majestic views of Positano with vibrant colors arching up the hillside and water so wholesome you would have thought you'd found the fountain of youth.

His delight was only heightened with each activity he bestowed on me. I wasn't going to give him the pleasure. He lingered his hands across my face and then awkwardly down my breasts. I hope he was getting off, as I wasn't going to forget this. This must have been the first time he'd ever done that to a woman, as a 12-year old boy could have done better on his first go. I guessed he had a needle dick. Or no dick. He must have sensed something

21

was up, as he stopped before he got to my nether region, and went upstairs.

The next person I saw was my pal Jake, followed by Steve. Two of the best Navy Seals out there. I'd been on different missions with them and was in awe of their abilities. True badasses, but human, too. I'd trust them if I was ever in a situation.

Jake looked at me and calmly said, "Dang, looks like we missed this invite."

"Shut up and untie me, fool. About time your weak asses made it here. Fuckhead was about to mallet my other foot, so you get the prize of carrying me out of here."

Steve now chimed in: "Always having to cover or carry your ass, that's why they pay us the big bucks. Or, wait: we don't get paid the big bucks; you do, so you're buying tonight."

"Big shocker there. I'm taking it you missed him."

"Sorry, Matti, we couldn't confirm the situation, so it was either you or him. Good news: we flipped a coin and you won," Jake said with a smile as he continued to untie this sick bastard's knots.

"You're killing me, Smalls." I loved working with these boys.

And now, years later, here I was one foot away from this evil, sadistic, no-good terrorist.

Our eyes fixed on each other. No movement. He had a Heckler and Koch P30L aimed at me. I knew he wasn't going to shoot through the damn window at me, but then again, you couldn't reason with crazy sick fucks. He opened the door slowly, as he knew I didn't have anything on me, and continued with his aim at my forehead.

"Well, hello, Matti. How have you been?"

"Good, good. In fact, NEV-ER better."

"It's been a long time. I thought of you A LOT over the years. It was hard to find you, but I knew you couldn't have died over there, despite all the reports otherwise."

"Well, aren't you special? Bless your heart, if you had one."

"Why don't we take this inside and finish where we left off? Wouldn't want the neighbors to know who you really are. How's the husband and kiddos?"

My blood boiled. Time just ran out. I looked at Miguel, my heart beating, and calmly said, "Sure, Miguel," and then I whistled.

He didn't have time to react. He didn't have time to shoot. Hell, he didn't have time to blink.

Bruiser and Koda came from opposite sides, and dang, could those dogs leap. Damn, I wished I could have videoed this for other training ops. Bruiser had Miguel's shooting shoulder (or what would be left of it) while Koda went straight for the jugular. These pups. I gave Bruiser his name as he was the calmer, calculating type and people would mistakenly think he wasn't a killer. I wanted him to seem more menacing. Koda got his name from the movie *Brother Bear*. A loveable pup. He definitively was more personable and mischievous, and the younger of the two.

Now, I told you that they only *needed* to know 3 commands. Play, Alert, Attack. Didn't mean they don't know other commands. When I bent down and unleashed them, I simply said, "Circle Back." They knew what that entailed. They had been patiently hunched in the bushes that aligned the driveway waiting for the right moment. If they had sensed I was in imminent danger, they would have made their move sooner.

Koda had Miguel's limp-ass body still in his mouth, giving me the eyes. He wanted a snack. I wasn't necessarily expecting ol' Miguel here so quickly, and would have wanted to take my time on revenge and feed him, in pieces, to the fish in the pond, but guess I'd just have to do it post mortem. I had to get rid of this car, too; and do it quickly.

I looked at the dogs and simply said, "To the pond." Koda looked at me, defeated but obedient. Each grabbed one of Miguel's hands in their mouths and then did an Iditarod sprint to the back of the pond.

"I'll be back." Then I yelled back Koda's favorite command: "Snack."

And with that, Koda went to town.

Chapter 3
Training Day

By the time I finished 8th grade, I had already completed my high school course requirements and was doing advance placement classes in Calculus II and Trig. Miss Peterson turned out to not only tutor me in the academics, but outside, as well. She was like a damn combination of all the ladies in *Hidden Figures.* I begged my parents to let me go to any special training facility, but being only 14, then, no one was going to let me in because of my age. Plus, the parents wanted me to have a "normal" upbringing. Little late for that, don't you think? Plus, it was challenging for me to be around other people. It literally hurt my head to talk to most others. I envisioned me punching them in the face every time they talked. Tell me that was normal?

I continued to take dummy classes at school under pretense of being a normal high school student and skipped two grades, since I had met all my requirements. Mississippi. Just saying.

Which direction to go? College? Air Force Academy? West Point? Specialty programs? CIA? DEA? Turned out you must be 17 to join the Navy Seals, 18 for the CIA, 23 before you can go to the FBI Academy, 20 to be in the US Army Special Forces (Green Beret, Night Stalkers or Rangers). There was the Marines MARSOC, too. Oh, one BIG obstacle here. Most of these didn't take women, at the time. My mother started later than me; that was how she was able to go Quantico, and was one of the first females admitted. I wasn't going to wait.

By the time I finished high school, it behooved me to consider the location of these training camps. Most likely it was Kentucky or California. Stop it, we already knew the answer. Not that I was going to be able to know the difference at either location.

As luck would have it, my pal Freddy would play a big role in my next move. Turned out that the private sector didn't have the same age or gender requirements for training. Also, it turned out that Kentucky would look damn good versus 45 minutes outside of Minot, North Dakota, where I was heading.

My parents were not happy with my choice for me to leave to train at such an early age, but also understood that this was my calling and they couldn't stop me. I must admit it was a teary goodbye for all of us. I promised to call often and come see them when I could.

There were only two of us in this 4-year program, with the objective to train, educate, prepare, and condition for deployment for any special mission. It took a combination from the best of the best. Think *Top Gun*, but mixing all the military branches, with each phase focusing on instruction from land navigation, language proficiency, aviation, combat, etc. Forty-eight months of grueling instruction under the lead of retired Master Gunnery Sergeant Otto Wilson. Remember Dolph Lundgren in *Rocky IV*? That was Wilson, but older. From the looks of his face, he'd been on the losing side of some battles. By the looks of his arms, and the fact that he was still standing here, he'd had his fair share of wins, too.

I don't know why, but I was expecting to see a dude walk in to be my companion for the next 48 months. I naively didn't consider that if I was here, most likely it would be another female, too. I assumed "Uncle" Freddy had just hooked me up. Lesson number 1. Never assume.

I still recall her face, when she walked through the door. First thought: Robin Givens in *Boomerang*. She was drop dead gorgeous. Flawless skin; looked like a runway model. I was good looking, make no mistake, but she looked like she came from money. Turned out, she did, and that was her connection in. But there was more. She was a physical beast of a specimen. 5'9," no fat, tiny waist, toned athletic legs, a bit of a backside, and hair that was thick and flowing. And to top it off, she smelled like heaven. To this day, I don't know how she gets whatever scent she uses to last so long. She was damn near perfection. Bitch.

Our eyes locked as we sized each other up. Who's going to flinch first? Game on, let's do this. What seemed like eternity was broken when she had her left eye do this lazy eye, circle back thing in her head. Friggin creepy. I chuckled and so did she. So, she had a sense of humor. I knew just then we would be best friends for life.

"I'm Bethany."

"With a y or an ie?"

"With a y," she said.

Thank the Lord. Couldn't take another messed-up spelling, although in truth, me coming from Mississippi, I was thinking her name might be Mo'niqe or LaQuisha.

"I'm Matti. With an i. My parents wanted me to always be *special.*"

With that, we both laughed.

Bethany and I had an unhealthy, but humorous, competition between us. We pushed each other and we both had our own natural physical and mental abilities. If we were riding stationary bikes, she could peddle faster than the energizer bunny. I told her it was unfair: she had a bigger butt and it gave her more momentum. When we swam, I could do the length of the pool without breathing with no problems, and she'd tease and say it wasn't fair, since my boobs were like buoys (which made no sense to me, as that would make it harder, but who was I to correct her? I feared "Whop Eye" kicking my ass). She excelled in aviation, I in weaponry. Bethany was more trusting, I was more skeptical. She beat me in the 200; I beat her in the mile. She called me 'white girl' when I shimmied, and I gave her grief that she was only black person who couldn't double-dutch. We complemented each other completely.

There was one thing both us didn't have experience in....men. By 20, Command knew that most of our undercover missions required actual experience in how to seduce men. Not that we were going to be prostitutes, mind you, but we needed to know the gist of what to do. We learned how to drink (and I swear Bethany had a hollow leg, as she could pound them back) and we were instructed on how to "pick up" men, not that it required real effort, since we were both knockouts. Neither one of us at the time had any interest in a relationship, as we were dedicated and now programmed to fight for injustice and for others who couldn't fight for themselves. Plus, we had each other. Hell, we finished each others' lines and took food off each others' plates. We sure did know how to make each other laugh, but no, we weren't into each other that way.

When Gunnery Sergeant Wilson was berating us for something, she'd turn to me and throw that lazy eye and stick out her teeth in reference to him and make this nasty pussy face with her tongue. I know the military had a dental plan, but he obviously didn't use it. It cracked me up every time.

Four years. It was a long time to train with just one other person. Most people don't realize Minot Air Force base was a major strategic command base with both nuclear-tipped ballistic missiles and manned bombers, and was developing into a global strike command center. The 5th Bomb Wing was located there. This base was one of only two that operated B52 bombers. Because of the harsh winter conditions, other special forces came here to practice drills for combat; that helped us pick up additional special tactical skills and we made a few new friends along the way.

Bethany and I were like twin Bridgett Fondas in the *Point of No Return.* Our first deployment had us relocate to Los Angeles and our cover was being international flight attendants for Delta Airlines ("Building a better airline, not just a bigger one.").

This was supposed to be an easy in-and-out. Fly to Zurich. Go to gala, meet rich men, identify the main one, invite back to room, drug him, get info he had on him, and take anything in his room. One of us would be the seducer; the other the earpiece and control. I changed my eye color to brown, with contacts, for our first mission.

Get the information, leave. Get the information, leave. Easy peasy.

Our target went for Bethany. His name was Alexander Klauser. He was known for human sex trafficking all over Europe, with a penchant for trafficking arms, as well. Europe was a key location for both of these because of the weak border control and distance from destination countries and corrupt officials.

The event was being held at Baur au Lac, a resort that had a reputation for catering privacy to its discerning guests. The majestic views overlooked the Alps on one side and there was high-end shopping on the other. The ballroom and outside grounds were transformed with crystal chandeliers and centerpieces to illuminate the night to make it even more spectacular. Turned out, Alexander had particular taste. He was a Val Kilmer lookalike from *The Saint*, but hot like Val was, in that movie: he had a scar on the left side of his face that made him angry to be alive. He scoured the room, looking for his next conquest. Think revenge fuck, with more perversion. You could sense he wanted to inflict pain onto someone else—his pain. Other women in the room were begging for it, too. How pathetic. Did they not realize? Have you no pride in yourselves? Jesus.

It took two drinks before Bethany had him heading up. She'd learned how to work it, and was a natural. While she worked that angle, I slipped out and started doing my own reconnaissance. We had previously placed outside "eyes" on where we expected he'd take her. I communicated through her ear bud and only used taps if I thought he was in hearing range. Our plan to get the info and get out quickly went awry when he headed to the other side of the hotel wing versus going to the corner penthouse suite he had been accommodating.

Alexander grabbed Bethany as he headed up the east stairwell to the hotel rooftop, telling her he wanted to show her the stars. Something wasn't right. He was either on to her and would throw her off it, or was going to rape her and leave her there, dead. Either way, 'dead' was the key word. There was no other option. Couldn't reason with crazy. Man sold people and guns, so we could throw out mistaken intentions. Bethany was giving me clues to her location as she told him to stop squeezing her wrist so hard as they walked up. Once they entered the rooftop, Bethany tried to suppress the mood and make it more light-hearted, but Alexander seemed to be getting more and more agitated as he berated her on her attire, her hair, and her accent. She pulled away to look over the balcony and I was able to pinpoint her location.

Ninety seconds was all I had, by my best guestimate. I was already on the grounds, but had to retrieve my duffle, get in position, and get out of other peoples' view. I had a US Navy MK12 5.56 rifle with a silencer. I quickly moved across the grounds in 4-inch-high heels and gown and retrieved my bag, which was obscured by the heavy bushes that perimetered the open walkways. I then headed east another 150 feet before I was hidden by a massive Swiss stone pine tree. Bethany continued to provide location context clues, which Alexander must have caught on to, as he was now physically forcing her to the middle of the roof. Bethany was going to have to overtake him, or I was. I figured her cover was blown, regardless, so once I saw her head through my scope, I called an audible from *Top Gun* and told her if she couldn't take him, to break right at the count of 3 and head to the east side and start to climb over.

3
2
1
Break right.

Alexander chased Bethany to the side, as predicted. She pretended to launch herself over, and he grappled her to pull her back. That was my signal, and with that, I squeezed the trigger.

"Oh, that's gonna leave a mark," I told her through the earpiece.

"Did you just quote Chris Farley from *Tommy Boy*?" she exclaimed. "Good god. You need help."

"You're right...how about...BAM! Right between the eyes. *My Cousin Vinny* works much better, here," I replied. "You're welcome, by the way."

The mission was a fail on several fronts. We didn't get his suppliers, any additional information, OR coordinates. We did manage to take out the head of one sick organization.

Orders were to clean up and get out of there ASAP. That was the least of our concerns.

Command informed us we potentially were too identifiable by guests, and just like that, Bethany and I learned it was our first and probably last deployment together for a while.

(To top it off, thinking back, sometime later, we learned Chris Farley had died of an overdose. WTH?!)

Chapter 4
Lo Down

It was harder to get rid of a tricked-up yellow taxi cab than one might think. Remember: quaint East Texas. Not like I could just drive it down the block and ditch it. I drove it to Lake Palestine, a decent drive away and closer to Tyler, Texas which was a town big enough to actually have cabs, though I doubt they used them often. I listened to the Eagles and other old-time favorites on the drive...*Lighten up while you still can....and take it easy...*

I had a few steps to take care of, first, before I could dump it, which required no one to observe. For fun, I drove it into a tree on one side to make it look like it could have been a hit-and-run. I had to wait until early evening for it turn dark so I could make my next move of rolling it into the lake after I had wiped it down of any prints. Lake Palestine was about 18 miles long, so I had to identify a spot where no one would be watching from or near the lake. The lake was only about 50 feet in depth, so I had to make sure I picked the right spot for it to sink, or it would pop up and be identified too quickly. Location was key, because after I dumped it, I had to find a way back to the house, pronto. The eastern finger of the lake seemed to provide the best access point and the timing was perfect. On a vacated pier, I placed a large rock on the accelerator and watch it launch quickly off and then sink slowly into the water until it was engulfed. Step one complete.

I changed my pony tail to a bun and started jogging to Highway 31, which fed into Tyler. Had enough sense to bring my headphones, so I shuffled through more songs and prayed that some East Texas idiot wouldn't hit me on the side of the road as I made my way towards town. I shuffled through both Justins, LMFAO, and even Lady Antebellum. I had a 5-mile minimum commute to the outskirts of town, so I guess I was getting in my exercise for the day. Fucking Miquel. I wondered what Koda had left of him.

Once I arrived outside of Loop 323, I found a local Dairy Queen where I grabbed something to drink and hailed an Uber. There was no luxury XL available, but a black Volkswagen Golf came promptly and picked me up. It was clean, and the driver didn't talk much (probably because he had a wad of chew in his mouth and I could see the overfilled cup that he spat into). His teeth were yellow and brown and I wanted to shove a mirror in front of him. Guess there was not much to do in these parts. I tried to make myself blend in as much as possible; even bought a baseball hat to cover my head, and a large plain pullover. Numb-nuts drove me back to the outskirts of my town and dropped me off at the local high school with no questions in route. Bonus. Must have thought I was a teacher, which was fine by me. I made another fucking jog home and wondered what I was going to see.

Bruiser and Koda were on alert when I came back, and all was quiet on the home front. Miquel fared better than I thought, as Koda had just played with him. He could have passed for a part in *The Walking Dead,* with his insides hanging all out and one eye popped out and hanging by the optical nerve. I still have a chill when I think of that Negan character. Ran into a real-life Negan during my Fubar incident. Motherf'ers could all go to hell.

I now had to play *Dexter* and dismantle ol' Miguel here and feed him to the fishes. Come to find out Miquel didn't have anything to brag about down below, as I had long suspected. I cut that off first, to feed the fish. These fish were going to be well fed by the time I was done.

I dumped some of him into the lake with the remainder of the small bones to the fire pit and doused enough kerosene and pinon wood to make a mini bonfire. Damn, I was tired. I had no idea I was going to have to spend my whole day on this. I'd hoped to just relax and listen to some tunes and enjoy the fall weather before the real shit hit the fan. I turned on the outside radio and listened to Christian rock while I cleaned up. Yes, Christian rock. Get over it. I knew how that sounded, but, really, I just did the world some justice by taking Miquel out. Hal-le-lu-jah.

Thirty minutes later I got pinged by my high-tech security alarm that someone or something had breached the outer perimeter. I knew that if Miquel found me, my situation was compromised and the others would soon be coming, too. The bait had been taken. I took Miquel for a loner, so had hoped to have a little more time, but here we were.

I checked the video feed and saw my neighbor Gary walking down the driveway. Whew, that was a lucky break.

Gary was probably in his late sixties, 6'3, and a little portly in the belly, now, but you could tell he had been in good shape in his prime. He had gray, thick hair, blue eyes, wore Wranglers and boots, and drove a Chevy Dually Silverado 3500. I didn't see or talk to him much, but when I did, he always had a calm, introspective demeanor and you could tell he was genuinely concerned about me being here all by myself. He had an accent that I couldn't place. Not necessarily country, but one, none the less. At times, I'd catch him looking at me, and I'd swear I had seen him before. With so many missions and deployments, it was hard to not think everyone was out to get you.

I double checked to make sure nothing was out of place and went in towards the front door. I grabbed a watering can by the door and headed out. Gary approached, shouting down the driveway, "Well, what in tarnation are you doing at this hour?"

"Oh, sorry, Gary, hope I didn't wake you with the music and fire going. I just came back from a quick turnaround trip and couldn't get to sleep, so was trying to do a little yard work while I have it in me," I said.

"I saw some taxi pull up. Was that to take you to the airport? I could have taken you, or why didn't you take your little baby on this fine fall day?"

By baby, Gary was referring to my little love, the Jaguar C-X75. It was a two-seat concept car that was produced by the Formula One team, with 778 horsepower, even though hybrid electric. This one had a few extraordinary features, with bulletproof glass and an arsenal of weaponry that would make Bond quiver, all the while veiled in just a supped-up car. I knew I was trying to blend in here while I was preparing for next steps, but this little gem I could not resist, when I found it; thus, I rarely had the pleasure to take it out. Gary happened to see it, as he was a nosy neighbor.

"Have you ever seen the degenerates that park at private terminals? Nah, I wasn't taking a chance of getting my baby scratched up. It was no big deal to just cab it in."

"It looked like a pretty fancy taxi. Who did you call it from?"

"Hell, Gary, you need a new hobby to get you out of the house. I have no idea which company it was. I couldn't get an Uber out here in time to go, so just Googled 'local taxi' and they picked me up."

"Where are the pups tonight?"

Fuck. He sure was asking a lot of questions. This is why I stayed to myself. Bruiser and Koda were staring out the front windows, on alert. I left them in while I was talking to Gary, as I didn't have time to clean them up thoroughly and didn't want to have to explain, if he saw blood, that they'd just killed some possum or something out in the woods. Or, I could be truthful and say they'd just rag-tagged some sick fuck and we chopped him into pieces for the pond and lake and the pinon wood is masking the burnt flesh remaining on some dickless remains.

Or maybe not.

"Oh, they are a mess. I left them outside all day and they've gotten into everything. I really need to get them to a trainer. And a groomer."

Good god, shut up and leave, already. I faked a long yawn and stretched.

"Ok, well, didn't meant to keep you up any longer; just heard the music and saw the fire pit going and wanted to make sure all was ok."

"Thanks, Gary, I appreciate it. Sorry if I kept you up. I know your bed time is usually 9." And with that, I smiled and gave him a wink.

"Shut it, youngster. One day, you'll be my age, too."

I walked back inside and looked at the dogs. It was going to have to wait till morning. They weren't happy that I was making them sleep outside tonight, but they obeyed. I had other things to work on; namely my next move, as the clock had started.

Chapter 5
Amore

Bethany and I had spent so much time together, it was a blow when we learned we were going to be working solo, going forward, or with new situational partners. Situational meant someone new for each assignment. Trust was a big factor when working with someone, and even though we were trained to cover each others' backs, it's different when you must place your life on the line for a stranger.

We still worked together on occasional assignments, but were instructed that, for the time being, it wouldn't be in same location. We talked to each other several times a day. She was my life, my constant, my best friend, and the only family to me outside of my parents.

My next two assignments I did solo, which was just fine by me. No blood or guts, just reconnaissance, on these. I traveled from LA to Puerto Rico and then got another gig in Barcelona. I changed my hair and features to disguise myself. I was becoming very adept at it and chuckled, thinking I could always give this up and work in the entertainment industry.

While prepping for my fourth mission, I was in the Chateau Marmont bar sipping on a fine bottle of Dom Perrignon, Plentitude 3, 1983. I figured I deserved it for the success of the last missions, and since I wasn't footing the bill, why not? The hotel was modeled after a castle, and checking in was like visiting a European country estate, but with a perfect blend of old world charm and sleek sophistication. The bar was dark and mahogany and was known for the sex appeal to come make a deal – what type of deal was up to you, naughty or nice, as they promoted it.

I was there to observe a potential high-level threat whose true work was just coming to light. Seemed he was bringing information in and taking more out. I was to find out who he was getting it from and giving it to.

That's when my whole world turned upside down.

I saw him first. Tall, 6'5, and lean, like pure muscle. He was a friggin John Stamos look-alike. Could have been his identical, much taller twin. Model material. Black hair, piercing blue eyes, Greek decent. That jaw line. Damn, that jaw line. Those eyes. Made my knees weak just thinking about it. Big hands. Just saying. He was perfect.

He was wearing black jeans and a black v-neck shirt with a brown leather jacket. Just scrumptious. Not too made up, but not underdressed, either: just perfection. I caught myself staring way too long. He noticed it, too. He was with a group of people, all smiles and laughing. They looked like they were locals and frequented here often, most likely trust fund kids of some director or producer.

I nodded to the waitress to bring the bill. I needed to focus, and my prospect was on the move. I paid and was heading out the bar entrance when my arm was touched and I turned around.

"You can't leave yet," he said.

"Excuse me?"

"I'd be remiss if I let you leave without introducing myself. I'm Tom Baker."

"Well, Tom Baker. Nice to meet you, but I'm on my way out." My knees were buckling and I was keeping an eye on my target, who was now heading to his arranged transportation, all the while looking at this fine specimen in front of me. I knew I only had a few moments to pursue, or I'd have to pick up and track my target later.

"Please don't leave just yet. I'm sure you get this all the time, but I had to come over and meet you." His voice was perfect, too. Shit. Damn. In that second, I knew I was going to have to circle back to my target. I wasn't leaving that bar. Had it been pressing, I wouldn't have sacrificed it, but I knew where he was going and where to catch him next. Nothing would be compromised by me staying for a drink. Or two.

"Well, Mr. Baker, I'm flattered. Tell me, why is it you feel a need to meet me?"

He smiled. His teeth were perfect. Shit, shit, shit. "No beating around the bush with you, I take it? I guess that's why I felt compelled to come over here. I knew you are different just by looking at you. You are mesmerizing."

My mind was racing. Work, pleasure. Was this a setup? Odds were against it. Statistical odds of this leading to anything? Zero. What do I get out of it? Well, one night is better than zero. Couldn't hurt, right?

"If I may," he said as he grabbed my hand confidently into his and walked me back into the main area to sit down in a corner section. There was nothing foreign or strange about it. It felt like home.

"A little presumptuous, don't you think?"

"I'm not that way. You'll come to find that out about me."

We sat there talking for hours, just us, while we sipped on drinks. He shared everything about himself. He was a former tight-end for Alabama. (yep, Al-a-fucking Bama, so that was against him.) Blew out his knee in senior year and couldn't go pro. Business major. Masters at USC in psychology...of all things. California born and raised with ties to money. His parents and two siblings were killed in a plane crash when he was in school, so he was without any immediate family. He had recently opened his first workout facility that was a cross between weights, cardio, and CrossFit. Impressive clientele base, since he was located in the heart of Rodeo Drive. Smart move. He was confident but not cocky, open but not sappy, but the best trait of all was: he was outright just plain funny. Nothing more attractive than a man who could make you laugh. By the way he talked, you could tell he was a man of loyalty and honor. He was the perfect storm.

I shared bits and pieces of truthful information without divulging too much. Parents in Mississippi, attended private boarding school (well, if you want to call it that), came out here for work, only child – yadda, yadda. Technically, I wasn't lying about anything; just not going into specific details. I realized I hadn't been in a situation where I had to reveal much about my true self, and generally just got out of the situation if I needed to, but I didn't want to, in this case.

The bar was empty by now, with only us in there. Even though they have suggested closing times, Chateau Marmont prided itself on taking care of their guests. They would continue to serve us until sunrise, if we wanted, but we realized the time, and finally headed to the entrance to leave. I felt hesitant to leave, doubting my instincts for just an instant. This was more than just a friendly meet and greet. I felt it, and I knew he did, too.

Valet had left his car out front. A new, black, sleek Audi A8 with custom rims. It was all about the rims. (I hate it when people drop a load on a car and chinse out on the rims; it's so infuriating. Why bother?! Shame on any sales person who let them drive off the lot with it that way, too.)

He asked if he could drive me home and I said my work was keeping me here for a layover and I'd splurged on an upgrade to stay here. I jokingly said, "I'd invite you up, but I just met you." Who was I kidding? I wanted him. He was gracious and mature as he said, "Well, I'm not interested in a night, so I'll leave you here till tomorrow," and with that, he leaned over and gently grabbed my face with both hands and tilted it up. He pressed his lips to my forehead and said, "I knew from the moment I saw you. Tonight, my life changed forever. I'll see you in a few hours; get some rest, my brown-eyed beauty."

Damn, I wanted him. I knew I was in big trouble. I have blue eyes. Eyes and teeth were what I was attracted to. I looked at my reflection as I walked out, still incognito, for

our little pal that I'd now have to track down. I had Eddie
Money playing in my head... *Take me home tonight...*

Good grief.

Maybe he was a boob man and wouldn't care?

Chapter 6
All work and all play

It was not easy to work and play at the same time. While I had Mr. Dreamy Eyes on one side, I was there on a mission to track down what information was going in and out from Jacob Al-Hakam. I loved when foreigners paired an English name with theirs. Like when you go to the nail salon and their name is Nancy, only they pronounce it Yancy.

Al-Hakam translated to 'The Judge.' His eyes were soulless, and he had black wavy, floppy hair that hung below his ears, that he greased back and a mustache with an expanded goatee with sides that were unable to truly fill in. He was a smart dresser in a Gorgio Armani two-button soft basic navy suit with a Rolex that he wore on his right wrist. Slender, but not skinny. Maybe 5'10, and that might be generous. He actually had a decent smile, but his eyes were dead giveaway: he was never happy. He conversed easily with others, but never lost attention of his surroundings. Extreme paranoia? Or, cognizant of consequences?

Jacob presented himself as a self-made wine entrepreneur with vast library of Rothschild, Domaine, Chateau Margaux, and Lafite - all for sale for a price. Even had bottles autographed by former presidents. Interesting what people would spend money on without having to research it. They'd trust a stranger to inform them of a value. They'd store this precious bottle in their secure vaults, never to even open it, but just to say they own it. This was when it was important to understand the true importance of a knowledge of history. Presidents a hundred years ago couldn't autograph a bottle with the pens we have now. It all came down to the little details.

Being in Los Angeles with bigwigs and try-hards, Jacob had the perfect cover. With a little digging, with some help from friends in agencies, we discovered his ties to Al-Qaeda, buried, but not deep enough. He was the great grandson of a former leader, killed by Seals when his country took American hostages. America secretly retaliated when they sent Seal Team 6 in and killed the whole wedding party, hoping to put a stop to any legacies going forward, while sending a loud message. Baby Jacob was not there that day. His real name was Ramzi, which equated to 'the man who kept secrets.' Just great: I now had to tail a man whose real name was Man Who Kept Secrets plus Judge Whose Whole Family Had Been Mowed Down. I pictured a *Rambo* quote from him of *"They drew first blood, not me,"* right before he goes postal.

America was in a volatile period; thus the need now for independent contractors like me and others that had leeway to get things done without having to be buried in red tape or seen in the public eye. Of course, there was a down side. If anything happened to us, no one would be the wiser.

Ramzi traveled back and forth from LA to all over Europe, masqueraded by his wine explorations. This was what brought up the red flag in the first place. He didn't always return with wine in tow, so again, the details could be a killer. The US wanted to know what information was being transferred in an effort to thwart any terrorist attacks planned for LA or elsewhere.

Ramzi had a private tasting in three days, scheduled for thirty people. How was I going to follow/track/monitor him 24/7 and allocate time with Tom? I knew this couldn't work, but was determined to find a way, and that was when my break came. There were only 63 rooms in Chateau Marmont. Jacob was in the one-bedroom penthouse, while I opted for the garden cottage. He ordered room service the following morning for breakfast, consisting of crab benedict, a pressed smoothie, and a mimosa. By that, I knew he wasn't having or expecting any company. Timing was going to be crucial, so I quickly put on my workout clothes and made my way to intercept the room service delivery.

The hotel certainly lived up to their reputation, as the food came up precisely 25 minutes from when he ordered. The entrée was covered, but the juice and mimosa were on the top left corner of the tray the server was carrying. I had headphones on to an iPod and pretended to be struggling with the strap on my arm. As the waiter came closer, I feigned stumbling and conveniently swayed into him, making him stop to miss me, and I swiftly deposited half an ounce into the pressed juice without him noticing. It didn't hurt that I had a pushup sports bra on, which helped with the distraction.

Ol' Ramzi wasn't going to be going anywhere for the next 2 days. I'd put a high-level concentrate in his juice. He was going to be hugging that toilet from both ends. My guess was he'd think the crab was bad. Regardless, I knew he wouldn't be mobile and would be praying to Allah after this. Now I had some room to play.

Tom called mid-morning and said he'd wanted to call earlier, but felt bad that he had kept me up so late, and figured I'd be tired. Little did he know, bless his heart. He asked if he could take me to lunch at noon. Told him I needed to shower, as I'd just finished working out. He wanted me to stay as I was, as we'd be walking, to get some exercise. Interesting. Nonetheless, I cleaned up a bit, spruced up my messy bun, put on a tight cover, and listened in on Ramzi, who was already hitting the commode and, by the sounds of it, might literally be dying, based on what I heard. I was good to go.

I waited out front of the lobby for Tom to pull up, and this time he came in a white Range Rover SV Autobiography Dynamic. Hmm, nice taste. He pulled it up to the valet and got out, looking just as fine as when I left him hours ago. His muscular arms and legs were visible in his athletic gear of LuLuLemon. He wasn't made up, and I think that made the attraction even more intense. He looked this damn good in plain workout clothes. *Concentrate, damn it.*

He leaned in for peck on the cheek and grabbed my hand. "Glad you're still here and didn't run off."

(Fat chance.) "Well, I thought about it, but didn't have anything better to do today," I said with a smile.

His smile was contagious.

"Where do you think you are taking me?"

"I thought we'd enjoy this rare, perfect, glorious day in LA, and I know a place not far from here."

He wasn't joking. We literally left the resort, made two turns, and found our way to Pinches Tacos, which boasted Real Mexican Food by Real Mexicans.

"Glad to see you're not trying to impress me—or wait; being a psych major, maybe you are?" I teased.

"Only the best for you. I was too busy trying to impress a girl last night, and didn't eat much, so I'm starving. You'll love the pulled pork tacos."

Was it fate or coincidence that he'd brought me to a Mexican food place? Growing up in Mississippi, I'd had my fair share of barbeque. Not that I minded it: just had it all my life. I could eat Mexican food for every meal. We stuffed ourselves with tacos, asada fries, and little estiffy, which are little mini-chimichangas. He laughed, saying he was impressed that I cleaned my plate. Hell, I didn't eat last night, either.

We sipped on water and continued to converse on everything—world events, politics, religion. I waited for him to bring up abortion, next. You know: topics they generally told you to steer way from. Tom and I shared much of the same philosophy on everything we discussed and he had this unnerving ability to be so damn good-looking and personable while doing it. *Concentrate, concentrate, shit, shit, shit.*

Tom was 6 years older than me. I asked him why he wasn't married or involved and he divulged that he was married for a brief time, to his college sweetheart. Turned out she wasn't so sweet after all, and left him after 9 months to pursue someone with deeper pockets.

Understandably, he was a little gun-shy after that, and explained why he was resolute in making a name for himself with this new venture. Didn't need to be a psych major to see that.

We took our time and leisurely strolled back to the hotel. Tom asked how long was I staying here. Just a few more days and then I'd have to do an international trip for work and would be gone for roughly 10 days. Three days was all I had to see where this would go. The clock was ticking.

Tom had to go meet some clients, but asked if we could do a late dinner. That was perfect by me, as I had to do a little work, myself.

Back at the Chateau, I rewound and listened in to Ramzi, who was still at it in the bathroom. All good on that front. No calls made. No visitors. I then did a little research on his guest list and tried to determine if there was any angle for getting invited. All the guests were staying at the Chateau and appeared to be couples, with two spots not listing names but noted simply as 'reserved.'

I was going to have to work on Ramzi to get included, but poisoning him put a little hindrance in my initiatives. I had another night before I had to work miracles, so continued my exploration of anything I could find on him. While I was at it, I did a quick check on Tom, too. Could never be too careful, and all his info came back as he stated.

I called Bethany and filled her in on everything. She told me to ditch the new dude—that was until I had her pull up his profile. Her tone quickly changed to "tap that shit and then get out." Damn, she's funny; sure do miss seeing her every day.

Tom picked me up promptly at 8:30pm. He was wearing a white polo with a steel blue blazer and pressed jeans. Oh my. I had selected a little gold dress that had bared my shoulders. It had a plunging neckline and a t-strap in the back so my whole back was exposed. Not too shabby, if I said so myself. I had a Kim Bassinger look going on in *L.A. Confidential*, but racier.

I asked where we were going and Tom said it was a surprise. We drove about 20 minutes to Toluca Lake. Trendy little area right by Warner Brothers Studio and Universal. One main street with restaurants, cafes, and vintage stores. He pulled into this quaint, light blueish-grey house, lined with colorful flowers with a huge whispering willow in the front.

"We're here," he said. "Hope you're going to like it."

I must admit my first thought was, *really*? He got out of the car, opened my door, and grabbed my hand. The walkway was made of limestone and crushed granite with softlight landscaping lights that curved to the front door, which was a huge mahogany one-piece with wrought iron over a peek-through glass center. He opened the door to this large, open great room, which combined the living, dining, and kitchen. There was plenty of room for visiting guests or hosting parties in this elegant home. The back opened with 3 glass doors to a cascading waterfall fountain with a slender lane pool adorned with festive lighting in the trees. This house was deceptive and much larger than what appeared from the street. I had pulled his address, but didn't pull a visual on it. There were dark hardwood floors throughout the home, light custom cabinets, and white marble countertops with a built-in fridge. A huge white stone fireplace stood to one side. His master was on one side, with an office off of it, and he used one of the rooms for a workout area. He had three and a half bathrooms, all with updated and nice vanities, and another third guest bedroom that was almost idyllic.

As I looked around, I asked: "Who's your decorator?"

"Ha, that would be me. Do you like?"

(Take me NOW.) "Not too bad; mildly impressed."

"Oh good, I was hoping for 'mildly.' Anything more would just feel wrong." He smiled those perfect pearly whites.

"Please come outside. Since it's a nice night, I thought we could eat out here." He had a beautiful teak wood table, set up with white linens, fresh flowers, and chilling wine. Holy shit. There was a fire pit nearby, which was at the perfect temp.

"If you tell me you cooked a 5-course meal, I'm going to walk out. That's just showing off." I laughed nervously.

"I didn't cook, and trust me: you don't want me to cook. I was busy with my clients till late, so I hope you don't mind that I took the liberty of having someone serve us tonight."

As he pulled out my seat, two waiters came and attended to us promptly, pulling out my napkin to lay on my lap and filling our water and wine glasses. I could seriously get used to this. There weren't 5 courses. Only 4. No joke. We started with an arugula salad with a champagne vinaigrette, followed by a frothy potato soup, rosemary roast chicken with grilled asparagus, and a dreamy posset for dessert.

We talked and laughed about local news, recent movies, and what it was like living in LA. After my second glass of wine, I finally asked, "You go all out like this for all the ladies?"

He looked at me—right at me, like I felt it burning through me. His eyes were honest and sincere. "No, never have, actually. Haven't found anyone until now that I'd want to spend time with like this. I didn't mean to go overboard, but it was too late to get reservations anywhere nice and I did want to make an impression on you. I wanted you to know this isn't something just casual for me, and I hope it's not for you."

Dang, he wasn't making this easy. I looked at him for a quiet second, and took a long breath. His eyes looked a little defeated. I got up, moved him and his chair away from the table, and sat in his lap. My hands draped around his neck, I gently went in for a long, slow kiss: the kind that lasts for days, as Kevin Costner said in *Bull Durham.*

He drove me back home around 12:30. Yes, I was surprised, too, by our ability to leave without consummating anything further. We curled up by the fireplace and finished talking and drinking wine. He wasn't looking for a one-night stand, and I had to determine where, if anywhere, this was going to lead. I was more like Geena Davis in *The Long Kiss Goodnight*, having to tell a new boyfriend that I was a private contractor defending our country, who'd recently splattered a man's head on the rooftop. (I mean, he deserved it, but that was not the point here.) Little details like this tend to change people's minds about things. Not to mention, it was not like I could tell him a lot of details, anyway.

He asked if he could walk me up and I told him that wasn't necessary. He kissed me one last time before I got out and said, "Get some rest, brown eyes. I'll see you tomorrow."

Fucking contacts. My head was starting to hurt.

Chapter 7
Breakdown

When I got back to my room, I checked on the patient and he was sound asleep, snoring. Checked the logs and he didn't make any phone calls; none came in. Only one food service order, and that was Canada Dry ginger ale and some saltines. I researched further into the guests to see where the connection was. One by one, I started noticing a trend. After purchasing wines from Ramzi (aka Jacob), three of the couples had been robbed. Living in LA, that might not mean too much in terms of a connection, as odds are odds, but what was interesting was that, in each case, the robbers had stolen goods, jewelry, and...wait for it... wine. Money was untouched in each of these cases, which meant that robbery wasn't the motivation.

Why would they steal back potentially forged bottles? Well, if they were forged bottles in the first place, by stealing them back, no one would be the wiser and he could continue to operate in this industry and even resell the same bottles. Seemed like too simple reasoning, and there was also the potential for being identified for fraud. There must be another reason or more to the angle. What if they were transferring messages and information inside the bottles? Possibly in the boxes they were delivered in? Nope, that couldn't be it. They didn't steal the boxes. In the bottle themselves? No, what if one of the buyers actually drank the wine versus using it as a showcase? What do you do with opened vintage bottles? You put them on display. That left the cork or the label, and there was no telling if they kept the cork with the bottle if they did open it, so that left the label. It would be easy to mask a chip or embed messages on a fake label. By selling to innocents, there was no connection. The robberies all came at different intervals, seeming like someone could be very patient.

Patience wasn't necessarily my God-given gift.

I woke in the morning, ate breakfast, then got dressed in a black little number that would turn heads. It was way too early in the day, so I had to be careful not to be noticed by too many people. I went for Ramzi's room and knocked on it. When no one came, I knocked again. It took a second, but I heard a muffled voice say, "How can I help you?" I replied, "I was sent to help you."

He was depleted and weak as he opened the door and looked at me, confused.

"I'm sorry, I didn't order anything."

I looked at him and feigned embarrassment and said, "Oh my apologies, I hope I didn't disturb you. I must be at the wrong room."

He eyed me for a second, then said, "Wait, I recognize you from the bar the other evening. You were alone, though, drinking a nice bottle of Dom, if I recall correctly."

"Well, how observant. I do enjoy fine things. I was there waiting for a...client."

"What line of business are you in?"

"Have you ever seen the movie *Pretty Woman* with Julia Roberts?"

"Yes," he said, now more intrigued and apparently perking up.

"I'm like Julia, but higher paid and more polished. I know the difference between a Rothschild or a mere Jordan, can converse with anyone, and know how to eat escargot," I said casually and with a wink.

"I'm sorry. I failed to catch your name," he said as he extended his hand to shake mine.

"It's Naomi. Naomi Harris. It's been a pleasure to meet you; and again, my apologies for any inconvenience."

With that, I let go of his grip, turned towards the hallway, and started to walk away.

3.2.1.

"Excuse me, Naomi."

I turned around leisurely. "Yes?"

"If you don't have another engagement tomorrow night, would you like to accompany me to a private wine tasting that I'm hosting here at the Chateau?"

Thus, why you shouldn't think with your dick.

"What time?"

"At 7 pm sharp. The back of Bar Marmont has been reserved for it."

"One question," I said.

"What to wear?"

"No, I think I can handle that. What is your name?"

He laughed on that and then winced a little. I was hoping he didn't just squirt in his robe. "I'm Jacob."

"See you at 7:00 sharp, Jacob. I'm looking forward to it." And with that I continued walking down the hallway.

I hurried the rest of the way when I was out of sight, hoping to avoid anyone. I made it back to the room and undressed and put on some jeans and a t-shirt. I listened in and Ramzi was back in the bathroom. I had him isolated for about another 12 hours, by the sounds of it. I didn't think he was going to take any chances going out.

Tom called and asked when he was going to see me again. He knew this was my last night before I had to "travel" for work. Told him no fancy dinners, let's low-key early with drinks, somewhere quiet. He picked me up in the Audi and brought me back to Toluca Lake to a small bar/restaurant close to his house, literally within walking distance. It was 5:00pm and the atmosphere inside was dark. Like, pitch black dark. We huddled over to a corner booth and ordered a bottle of Shafer Hillside Select to share, and a grilled artichoke to nibble on.

He asked about my upcoming trip and why I had to be away for so many days. Told me he wasn't sure if he was going to make it and was considering how he could join me, if that wasn't too presumptuous. My head was reeling. Telling lies and working up aliases for work was one thing, but this was different. I thought about my mother, who I never knew. She was older than me when I was born. Had it been a one-time fling, or did she finally find the one, before she was killed? Whatever happened to her, she'd stayed alive long enough to deliver me. This line of work was not conducive to relationships. What was I doing here?

We continued to talk and sip, ordering another appetizer to share. I looked at this man in front of me with absolute awe. It wasn't just that he was physically beautiful, which he was, but he was kind, generous, thoughtful, smart, and funny. He was the true thing. I was a fake.

I had two choices and neither was good. I could tell him and rock his world, most likely never to see him again, or I could just leave and never return, potentially rocking his world just as much. The first option, he could cope with easier. It would be about me, not him, and hopefully my identity would not compromised going forward. The second option would be easier for me, but would leave him wondering and self-doubting. I guess there was a third option, where I slept with him and then killed him so he'd be none the wiser. (Stop it, that wasn't happening).

After we finished the first bottle, I suggested we return to his house. His eyes captivated, he walked more confidently. He was hesitant as he opened the door, contemplating what to do next. He walked in, turned on the foyer light, and turned around to find me undressing him with my eyes, wanting him to take control so I could lose control. This was going down.

He walked over to me and put his hand around the back of my neck and pulled me in. He lingered as he stared into my eyes, making me want him more. He angled my neck and slowly started to kiss it from the bottom, working up to my mouth, breathing in and intoxicating the moment. My pulse rose, wanting him. His kiss was slow with intent, soft but forceful, a perfect mixture of pleasure and lust. Knowing I couldn't take it anymore, he picked me up as I wrapped my legs about his taunt torso and carried me to the bedroom.

The rest was mind-blowing and numbing. You know you should keep some things private, so let's just sum it up with, *Oh my fucking god*. You can get the visual. We were spent, but fueled, over and over. Minutes turned into hours and time was lost and found, finally giving up to exhaustion and utter fulfillment. It was heaven.

We both fell fast asleep, in a dream-filled state. I woke depleted and dejected by my next move. Depeche Mode's *Somebody* was playing in my head...*I want somebody to share, But at the end of it all...(he) will understand me...*

It was almost dawn when I awoke from a deep slumber. I quietly got up and dressed, watching him and knowing I would never find this again. I went to his office to find paper and a pen, and wrote the following note:

"Tom, I am not who you think I am. You deserve the best. I am truly sorry – Matti."

I took off my contacts and left them on the note. I walked out the door.

61

Chapter 8
P.O.S

I needed to refocus. I was here for a specific mission: to find out what Ramzi was really doing. My heart ached as I thought about what Tom would think and feel as he read my note. I had to block it out of my mind or it would consume me. *Focus, damn it.*

I went back to the Chateau and checked on all my surveillance. All good to go. I called Bethany and filled her in. She was surprised by the direction I took and asked if I had considered all the options. I didn't want to go into it right then, and told her that I had to get this locked down with Ramzi.

I laid on the bed for a quick second and realized how exhausted I was physically, mentally, and emotionally. I took a power nap, as I knew I had to be rested and ready for the evening.

I awoke to my room phone ringing. Only Tom would be calling this number. I called down and requested to have my room unlisted. I would have changed rooms, but had all my equipment and surveillance already in place. Tom didn't know my room number, so I'd have to chance that he wouldn't try to locate me. I was leaving tomorrow; I couldn't afford any distractions.

By evening, I was prepped and ready. I wore a 3/4 long black form-fitting spaghetti string dress with Louis Vuitton stilettos, with my hair pulled up in a loose-fitting bun with ringlets flowing down the sides and back. I kept my jewelry simple with a diamond accent solitaire pendant necklace and matching earrings. For my watch, I selected a platinum and diamond Rolex Datejust in a presidential bracelet setting. Simple, but elegant: that was how I rolled.

I sauntered in at precisely 7:00 pm and turned every head in the room, including ol' Jacob/Ramzi. Ramzi came over to me and whispered, "Well, you certainly know how to make an entrance."

"Want you to get your money's worth. By the way, we can discuss my fee later. I'm sure you are good for it," I said, smiling, as I looked over at the guests and walked over to introduce myself.

I presented myself as an old neighborhood friend who happened to be in town, and I could tell Ramzi was appreciative that I took the initiative with a back story and wasted no time conversing with the group as we discussed the evening and recent purchases. I feigned delight and amusement as they recanted their stories and recent splurges. The couples there were considerably older than me, so I had to be cognizant of how I broached certain conversations. As part of my back story, my family grew up in the wine country and we owned a small private family label vineyard for a hobby, mostly, and were still just figuring out the dynamics of this complex industry. Interestingly enough, one of the couples, Jon and Sara Worthington, thought they'd heard of Harris Vineyards, the pretend vineyard I'd just made up. This tipped me off that they probably were the targets for the evening.

Ramzi was a smooth operator, knowing his audience and working them appropriately. You certainly wouldn't have suspected he was ass deep in the bathroom for the last 48 hours, or funneling information to known terrorist groups.

After 30-45 minutes of chitchat, we were directed to a more formal sit-down for Ramzi's presentation. Now, Ramzi really pulled out his charm as he presented vintage bottles for purchase. There were only 5 to select from: Chateau Margaux 1787, Chateau Lafite 1869, Shipwreck 1907 Heisieck, 1947 Chavel Blanc, and a 1992 Screaming Eagle Cab Sauvignon. The most recent Screaming Eagle was fetching the largest price because of the limited availability and production. The price range started at $200,000—not chump change, that was for sure.

Ramzi presented the wines to various couples he felt most likely to purchase them, except for the Screaming Eagle. He saved that for last and blatantly targeted only the Worthingtons. Jon and Sara were in their mid-fifties. He was a pudgy bald man, who over-compensated for his lack of physique with expensive clothes that still didn't fit right. She attempted to dress California chic, which came off more like those old ladies in the movie Titanic. Wrong era, wrong look. They had new money, and wanted to make others knew that they belonged. I watched in amusement.

One other couple feigned interest until the price went over $400,000, and at that point, the Worthingtons were the sole contenders. Hell, they outbid themselves as they finally settled at a cool half million. Ramzi would gross over $1.5 million when the night was done. Not too shabby. It was a $10K entrance fee per person just to attend. I wonder if any of these attendees understood they'd just fronted a terrorist act and organization, and most likely were buying two buck chuck?

After the auction was over, the couples sipped on other varietals and continued conversing. I moseyed over to the prize table to examine more closely the bottle of Screaming Eagle. It was standard dark bottle size, 750ml, with a red protective sleeve and a roughly 2x3-inch logo of a flying eagle. The logo had a small indention anomaly on the lower left-hand corner, which one may have thought was a simple handling or transportation miscue. To a more trained eye, it could be where someone attempted to lift to peel back or replace it. I continued to observe the bottle and the original wood box that it was shipped in. I casually put the bottle back when I noticed Ramzi coming my way. He put his hand on top of mine as I did so.

"You've taken quite an interest in this one," he said purposefully.

"Just curious what makes this one fetch the price that it did. Personally, I would have purchased the Lafite."

"You have expensive tastes, for your age."

"I'm not sure what age has to do with it. I prefer to think about it in terms of experience; and of that, I have plenty."

"I'm sure you do; it wasn't my intention to be demeaning. I'm looking forward to your experiences later."

(*I bet you are, you sick fuck.*) I smiled convincingly and nodded my head up and down. "Me, as well. For now, I'm hoping you can find someone to pour me another glass."

The problem with having these types of events was that guests would continue to stay as long as you served. Ramzi made a fatal mistake in not having a more formal end time. Of course, when buyers are dropping that kind of cash, you weigh your options. Jon and Sara were tying one on and announced to the group that they wanted to open the Screaming Eagle for everyone to try. The crowd cheered and I thought Ramzi was going to lose his shit. This confirmed my suspicions that this was a targeted bottle and buyer. Ramzi coolly suggested another fine vintage in its place and encouraged Jon and Sara to safeguard and treasure their newest investment, at least until all the paperwork was complete. Crisis adverted, but barely, as they were intent on showing the others that they could afford to open it now. Ramzi then insisted on having all purchases shipped to their estates by personal courier so they wouldn't be inconvenienced by carrying it. At this point, Jon and Sara were content with the offer.

The night wrapped up with everyone in full form. Once all the guests left, Ramzi had the concierge bring a cart over to take the bottles back to his suite with instructions that there was a million and a half dollars' worth there, so don't fuck up.

We lingered a bit, conversing about the evening as we made our way back to his suite. My time was coming to a head. I debated if I could drug him again without suspicion, but it was either put out or get out time. I wasn't putting out.

Once we made it back and the bottles made their way back, too, Ramzi started in full beast mode as he turned on the music, took off his jacket and tie, and went in for a bite on the ear. Not a nibble; a fucking bite. Like that would turn anyone on. Good grief. Times like this made me wish I would have selected another profession. Just then, remnants of my previous contact with him may have resurfaced, as he unexpectedly stated he had to go freshen up, quick. Thank you, Jesus. I scanned the room quickly for any weapons or other devices that could be used and made my way to the cart to investigate the Screaming Eagle more closely. I looked at the corner label to see if I could pull it back easily, and sure enough, it came up easier than it should. I was meticulously slow in trying, knowing my time was limited, too. I could see the letters ICB before I had to stop, realizing Ramzi was making his way out of bathroom. I patted the label down, hoping the edges would still stick.

Ramzi went over to change the music and it must have played from his personal playlist, as it was a profound instrumental piece. Kind of menacing in its tone, which set off my instinct that something was not adding up. I then stated that I needed to freshen up, as well, before our evening climaxed.

I head to the bathroom and turned on the faucet while I looked around. I listened at the door and thought I heard Ramzi typing on his phone. I looked at myself in the mirror, stalling, contemplating my next move. I turned around and my heart dropped when I saw a tiny camera on the vanity that was focused on the main room. He would have seen me with the bottle and had left this in here so that I would know that he knew. Holy shit.

Think, damn it. I had nothing in the bathroom that I could use. Not even a razor. He called out, asking if I needed any help. Shit, shit, shit. Not to be to repetitive, but the problem with crazy is that you can't reason with it. This man was a criminal either because he was born that way (understandable, since we ashed his whole family), was naturally insane, was a criminal by passion, or was a habitual or an occasional criminal (or in this case, he might just be all of these combined). When hit with confrontation, people froze, fled, or fought. Time to fight.

I took off my dress and opened the door. By the look on his face, I guessed Ramzi wasn't suspecting this option. I walked my way over to him—mind you, still in my stilettos. His eyes followed me, engulfing everything he saw. His mood was much more somber. He was playing out his options in his head, as well. I walked over to the counter and turned around and said, "How about you take me from behind from here? Is this a good height for you?"

He was obviously on to me, so I just had to hope he'd want to fuck me before he did anything. He took off his shirt as he walked briskly over and turned me around. Tick, tock. He grabbed my hair with his left hand and pulled down on it hard. I let out a little yelp before pushing him back. All the while, he was still holding onto my hair. By now, he was pulling me and leading me to another area of the room, directing me with my hair as he pulled down on it harder, forcing my neck to face up to the ceiling. He yanked some more before he got me over to the side table, opened the drawer, and grabbed with his right hand a small Kimber Pro Carry II handgun. Things were not looking up.

He continued his forceful grip of my hair in his left hand and was now yelling at me in broken English, asking what the fuck was I doing here and who did I work for? He continued with this short rant, all the while yanking my hair and threatening to pull the trigger. I was scanning the room for anything that might help when I saw our reflections in a mirror and remembered that his watch was on his right wrist. It all came down to the details, my fine friends.

The Kimber Pro was great for a concealed handgun, but it had an extra security grip safety which reduced the chance of an accidental discharge because you must securely and intentionally grip before you can pull the trigger. Ramzi was a leftie, so he naturally grabbed my hair with his dominate hand. Therefore, unless he was proficient at shooting with his right hand, he would have trouble firing this weapon. Time to find out.

A basic defensive move when someone was holding you from behind was to squat down, lunge back, and elbow the groin, all in one fluid motion. Don't be half ass about it, either: you're doing this to stop them; otherwise you are the next victim. 3.2.1.

I squatted, lunged back with my right leg, and stuck out my elbow, hitting his target. Ramzi didn't have a firm grip on the Kimber and therefore couldn't pull the trigger. He had to let go of my hair as he doubled over from the impact of my blow to his groin. This now freed me up to turn around and, with the palm of my hand, go for the final blow as I rammed it up his chin, forcing impact and knocking him onto the ground. The gun flew about 5 feet from where he landed, almost dropping at my feet. I picked it up slowly and aimed it at his head.

"I think it's time you told me more about your little operation, you fucking wack job."

Ramzi was wobbly as he tried to center himself on the ground. He fell straight down again on his chest. I noticed his hand had been in his pocket, and he shook his head violently, like he was trying to get the cobwebs out.

"Get your hands up and get up. Don't make me repeat myself."

He laid there. WTF? Guess he was going to make me do this the hard way. I sidestepped and kicked his head. He didn't move from it. Shit.

I waited to be sure, but already knew what I was looking at. I rolled him over and foam was coming out of his mouth. That wasn't from me. Motherfucker must have taken a fast-acting sodium nitrate tablet. At least he went this way, versus blowing us both to kingdom come.

I immediately reached for his phone and saw his last text to an unidentified number. It said "Our cover is blown. Wait for instructions."

I peeled back the label which read ICB and the next letter was smudged. ICBM? Intercontinental ballistic missile. Why write it out? Underneath was 33.9391 N, 67.7100 E. Longitude and latitude coordinates. I had a feeling of where, but couldn't confirm it off the top of my head. I knew my road trip was about to change.

I called for backup. I cleaned the room of any of my prints, took his phone, wallet, and bottle, put his clothes back on, and lugged him into an upright sitting position on the couch. This would have to do until someone else could finish it right. I put a "Do not disturb" sign on the door and walked out.

So many questions were going through my head. Why was he so quick to off himself? He feared worse retaliation? From whom? There had to be more to the bottle than what was written on the label. Was this a set-up? What were my next steps? This was a bigger operation than a one-woman pony show. I was going to have to call Freddy and get some help.

Chapter 9
Fred Meister

I'd been connected to Freddy since birth. I'd never met Freddy. He was like Charlie and Bosley in *Charlie Angels*, all rolled up in one. We were in constant contact, but I didn't know what he looked like or where he lived. He'd helped finance my life up to this point, along with whatever my mother set aside for my parents. He'd helped get me into my training. He identified assignments for me. He sent backup. We worked the case together. He was my command.

From his voice and conversations, the only thing I knew for certain about Freddy was (1) he was male (2) probably in his mid-late sixties (3) had a northern accent (4) had an unhealthy obsession with me. I often wondered if he was my birth dad. Why would he be so loyal to a woman's child, if not? But if so, how screwed up was it, that he would choose never to touch or hug this child? To be in this line of work, we all had our bag of serious issues.

I went back to my place in Manhattan Beach and changed into a long black wig and almost-black contacts and packed a bag. I traveled light, this time. I had a long flight in front of me, so had time to go over the contents that I was taking.

Freddy called me while I was on my way to the airport.

"You were right about the coordinates. Afghanistan."

"Hello. Glad you are ok, too. Do you need anything?" was my gentle reminder back to him.

"We don't have a lot of time. I've arranged private transport for you from LAX, which is taking off in 30 minutes. Make sure you're on it."

"Thanks, Uncle Freddy. Have anything more for me? Hate to go in blind, especially when there are unfriendlies."

"I have people going through his phone that you transmitted, and checking his place of residence now, plus we'll go through the bottle. Hope to have lots more by the time you land."

"Ok, I'll go through my end while on the plane and will send a report. I've got to get some shuteye, as I'm running on fumes."

"Sleep after you report. I called in Bethany to go with you on this one. Try not to kill everyone you encounter, this time."

(Hell yeah!) "Hey, that's unfair. I didn't pull the trigger on this bloke. How was I supposed to know he was skittish?"

"Your orders were to observe and relay, not participate and destroy."

"Just trying my best, boss."

"Did you just quote a Kurt Russell line from *Overboard* to me? We really need to get a psyche evaluation on you."

"What can I say; you watched it. Thanks for sending B on this, Freddy. I'll call when I land."

"Matti, is there going to be any blowback from your recent companionship?"

Holy shit. He was talking about Tom. How did he always know these things? I hadn't had any time to even think about that. Damn, now I had a whole ocean to think about it.

"Not sure what you are referring to. Line breaking up, chat soon."

Chapter 10
Road Trip

Double trouble. That's what we were. I felt like I was in
Stripes, when he said, *"There's something wrong with us,*
something very, very wrong." Damn, we were cute and
funny. I was so glad Bethany was meeting me. I needed
to unwind and get her perspective on things. She met me
on the runway looking perfect, as always. Bitch. It really
was annoying. I was not sure how she did it, but she
always looked on point. Just once, I'd love to see her all
sweaty and in disarray.

She came beaming up to me with a full perfect smile and a
mimosa for each of us in her hands. "Here's to however
you fucked up to land us this gig, cheers."

"Missed you too, girlfriend. May be a premature toast,
with this road trip."

We boarded a G6. Not a bad way to fly, if you ask me. The
G6 was capable of going 7,500 nautical miles, taking you
from LA to Melbourne, and was marketed as the fastest
and most expensive business jet on the market. It would
be a little out of reach to make a direct flight to
Afghanistan, but we were doing a stopover in London first
for supplies; both fuel and ammo from our partnering
friends. Not sure who Freddy hit up for these sweet rides,
but I liked it.

Bethany and I got situated and comfy with drinks as we
took off. I filled her in on Ramzi and everything I knew and
didn't know. We plotted potential next steps and

expectations. We were two hours into the flight before she asked me the real question.

"Well, are you going to make me ask, or are you going to spill it?" she simply stated.

"What do you mean?" My way of avoidance.

"Two guesses, and the first one doesn't count. Spill it. I want to hear about the Greek God you are obviously pining over."

"Ohh, you want to talk about that little nugget," I hedged.

"Well..." I filled her in on everything. We spent more time on this than we did national security, that was for sure. After I finished wrapping up and we'd bounced pros and cons, she looked at me and said, "Well, not to sound like my momma, but what's meant to be, will be, and this too shall pass." Jesus, thanks for that. With that, I went back and passed out from exhaustion.

By the time we got to London, Freddy had sent over what they deciphered from the bottle. The label was just one coordinate, etched multiple times all over the bottle. The label was the key to the other coordinates, but they were still unable to unlock the true significance of it all. It was like that movie with Jodie Foster and Matthew McConaughey in *Contact* where they were trying to decipher some cosmic code. We had coordinates for Iraq, Israel...and a few other "stans" as I called them (Kazakhstan, Pakistan). Trouble was, when you were being sent signals from all over kingdom come, you tended to think the worst. True terror was not necessarily physical; it was mental. Fear will crumble people and nations.

The phone was clean, with only that one number, which was traced to Turkey. So, that dictated our first stop. We were going to play cat and mouse and see if we could catch a rat.

There were some beautiful women in Turkey. Not a lot of black people, though, so Bethany was going to have to be my earpiece for this part. Women faced significant disparities in employment, religion, and education, along with being victims of rape and honor killings. Honor killings were usually committed by male family members against female members for bringing dishonor to the family. Could be for having sex outside marriage, denouncing faith, or because you got raped (probably by your brother...see note above). Needless to say, this country wasn't advocating for women's rights. To fit in, I donned a dark brown wig and dark brown contacts and covered up appropriately. Didn't want to look too nice, but at the same time, I hoped someone didn't want to tag team me in any circumstance.

We were outside their capital, Ankara, in a little town called Pursaklar. There were 19 condensed neighborhoods with various terrains. Our target hadn't moved locations in over 14 hours. I was sure they had a contingency plan in case Ramzi didn't resume contact. How much time they'd allow to pass was going to be the key to our next step.

When I was in position, Bethany texted the following to our mystery pal: "Clear. Time for next step." We had argued over what would tip them off, and settled for this gamble. We had no background or history of other communication between these two parties, so took risks by sending anything. Bethany had eyes in the sky and it showed only one heat-seeking body in the building. Didn't trust that the little bastards weren't hiding under some tarp, and didn't want to go in blind. Better to force them out onto more neutral ground (if you could even say that, since they at least would have the advantage of the lay of the land).

One, five, then fifteen minutes passed. Nothing. Heat sensors showed little movement and finally no movement when it reached 20 minutes. Then no heat was detected. Damn: our hands were tied, and I'd have to enter. I prayed a quick Hail Mary, as I feared this perp had booby trapped the place to blow. I couldn't bring my fav Colt, so checked the safety and silencer on the modified FNP90 that I was carrying under my traditional Turkish garb. The P90 was compact, but powerful and futuristic for the time. It has a unique top-mounted magazine with high-velocity custom 5.7mm ammunition that fragments on impact and distributes kinetic energy to the target alone. It's a beast. I was starting to really like it. I surveyed to ensure no additional outsiders were casing the joint and Bethany confirmed no other heat images were near. In condensed cities like this, I found that hard to believe. Almost like they knew not to be around. Definitely gave me a squeamish attitude for entering. I made my way to the door and tested it. It was locked, so this meant I was going to have to force my way in and pray for the best, if there was someone still inside waiting on me.

3.2.1. Didn't need full force to kick in this weak door. No lights. No movement. Something wasn't right, and that wasn't just because I was in Turkey tracking down who knew what. I cleared each room until I got to the last one. Mattresses on floor, and cheap couches littered the rooms. Sheer shades were used for window treatments. This looked like a typical home. Nothing stood out. Relayed to Bethany to look for any movement outside of perimeter. Backtracked quickly. How did he get out? Where was he hiding?

As I headed back to front door, there was a door I didn't originally see under the staircase. It had three locks on it. Suddenly, your typical house was looking not so typical. I slowly opened it as I inspected for any wirings or riggings. As I opened, I saw the steps leading down. No lights. I had a bad feeling about this; it made me think of *Silence of the Lambs,* where Stallings goes down to the dungeon to see the freak dancing with his dong between his legs. Needed to shake that visual out. Tried to relay to Bethany, but the signal was fading out as I went down. Turned on the light mount on my P90. It was bright enough to show me a path, would blind them from seeing me clearly, and would aid me, so they couldn't take an easy head shot. Nothing on the walls; it was literally a cave with a winding hallway. Was it rigged, or just used as an escape route? Had to go slowly, in case it was the latter. Where was it leading; how long was it? Easy to become paranoid.

The hairs on the back of my neck were standing up. Something was off. All living things, from complex mammals to single cell organisms, instinctively respond to danger. Our hearts pound, our palms sweat. I turned off my light and stayed put. Listening. Nothing. I slowly started backing up. I had a feeling I was about to pump 900 rounds down this narrow hallway and hoped to hit more than the wall. I was almost back to the staircase when I saw a small flicker of light growing. Oh, shit. I turned to the stairs and took them up by threes. I was out the front door when the explosion underground went off. Felt like an 8.2 earthquake, and the whole residence started to sink in. I was hightailing it down the street, with all kinds of shit falling from adjacent buildings. Bethany was in my ear, asking for a status update. WTF? Do you not see the sunken building or billow of smoke? People were out now, wondering what was happening. I now ducked and moved between buildings to make my way back, praising Jesus I'd turned off my light in time to be able to see what was coming.

Perp gone. Cave demolished. House in ruins. F' me. We didn't have time and wouldn't send units in to see what may or may not have been. Plausible deniability. If they were sophisticated enough to have a cave and the ability to blow, there would be nothing left for us to go off of in a timely manner.

Back to square one. Well, at least this time, Freddy couldn't complain about me killing anyone.

Bethany and I spent the next 10 days globetrotting and hitting the other coordinates, only to come up with nothing. It was a rope-a-dope.

Chapter 11
Turning Point

Flying back into LAX, I was suddenly apprehensive. I was returning after two weeks, in which time I gave no thought to the circumstances I'd left. I kept telling myself that it didn't matter. There was a sudden void and I understood that I had briefly encountered hope and lost it because of my unwillingness to accept that I was different. The song *Creep* by Radiohead played in my head...*But I'm a creep... I don't belong here...you're so fucking' special...*

Bethany and I hugged it out while we grabbed our things. She was already assigned to a new mission that would require her to do a quick turnaround. I, on the other hand, was on a wait and see basis. I was being scrutinized over my previous missions where, in either case, I'd killed the target or lost the lead/contact because of (what I would argue was) no fault of my own. This, too, would pass. I had proven my worth and I knew this was just a short delay.

I returned home and realized I had nothing to keep me there, so I started hitting the beaches. I hit Santa Monica, Malibu, Manhattan, Huntington, Long, and Newport Beaches. I played some pickup volleyball and rode bikes, grabbed some drinks with local strangers, and just hung out. Nothing worse than being with people and still feeling alone. Something had to change. I needed to snap out of it.

Three weeks home, and I was completely stir crazy. I was technically OOC. Out-of-commission. Best part of my day was when I heard from Bethany and she filled me in on her assignment. Told her how bored I was, and if I started whittling wood, to come shoot me. Her sound advice was to go hook up with a stranger to get my mind off things. Probably not bad advice, just couldn't wrap my head around it.

I was driving around listening to Fiona Apple singing *Criminal... I've been careless with a delicate man...when a girl can break a boy...*

Good grief.

Before I knew it, I realized I had driven to Pinches Tacos. What was I doing here?! I thought I'd keep driving, but then again, what were the chances? My hair and eyes were different, so even if there was a fluke encounter, he wouldn't recognize me. I was trained in this.

I went in and ordered the same thing as last time and sat down in the corner so I could survey everyone coming in and out. I ate slowly, taking my time. I was stalling; how pathetic. Finally, I got up to leave, deflated but relieved. As I opened the door to exit, Tom ran smack into me. Holy shit! I tensed, ducked my head down, avoided eye contact, and mumbled an apology as I continued walking past. My heart was racing—shit, I didn't get this worked up on assignments.

I walked a block down the road on Sunset Boulevard. I left my car in the parking lot, worried that I may have mentioned what model to him. How could I have been so juvenile as to go back there? If this man did have genuine feelings for me, I couldn't bring him in to my world. It wasn't fair to him. I passed by Starbucks and Trader Joes, and contemplated how much time I needed to be out before I returned to get my car and leave.

Damn, he looked good, too. I hit Laurel Lane and made a right, figuring I'd loop around towards Fountain before I headed back and surveyed the area. As I turned the corner, I heard, "Matti, STOP!" My heart sunk. How did he know it was me? My eyes closed and I stopped and turned around.

"I've been at Chateau Marmont every day, praying I'd run into you. They have you to thank for my bar tab. I've replayed every conversation in my head to the point that I surely need therapy. My work is suffering, but more importantly, I know I wasn't wrong about how we felt. Please tell me the truth about why you left so I can know and not have to wonder."

"Oh Tom, I am so sorry for what I have put you through. I know I shouldn't have come here today, but I'm sure my subconscious was driving me to this encounter. You are right that what we felt was real; it's just that you fell for someone that you don't really know."

By this time, Tom was standing within inches of me. He looked me in the eyes and grabbed my shoulders with tears streaking down his face. "I know you. I don't care what you have done or what you do to make you feel this way. I believe in us. Have faith in me. I know we are meant to be."

I did what any lovestruck person would do. I hit him. No, get real. I collapsed in his arms, cried like a baby, and told him I was sorry, all the while kissing his luscious, gorgeous lips. I was emotionally spent, but suddenly reenergized. I had found my hope again.

"Tom, there's so much I need to tell you. Let's go someplace quiet. You need to hear and know the truth so you can make an informed decision."

"Matti, before we even go there, I need to tell you something first." My heart raced. I'd had some bad juju luck going on, and I imagined he was about to tell me he had 5 kids with 4 different mothers, or got a tattoo of a skull on his pelvis during this period. Long breath in and out as I waited.

"I wasn't sure it was even humanly possible, but I find you even more attractive, with your blue eyes." Oh, thank you, Jesus!

We walked back to our cars, hand in hand, not saying a word. I followed him to his place. I rehearsed in my mind what I was going to tell him, and would probably not go into all the gritty details.

When we entered the house, he told me to wait. I heard him rummage through the kitchen and come back with a bottle of Cakebread chardonnay and two glasses. We sat down and he leaned over and gave me a longing kiss. "Let's hear it."

Trust was not necessarily my strong suit. I came into this world under ambiguous circumstances, which defined the path I selected. Defining moments. Think back to your first memory. Whichever one you can remember, defines you. I completely agree with this statement. I was abandoned, but under sacrifice. Loyalty and honor, but country came first. In a *Few Good Men*, he stated it was Unit, Corp, God, Country. Movie faux pax. It was God, Country, Corp, and if outside the military purview, one would argue it was God, Family, Country. Despite what you think, I was brought up deep Catholic, so not withstanding what I did for a living, it was embedded in me.

I decided to lay it all on the line. I told Tom about how I came to my aunt and uncle, who I called Mom and Dad; told him about my biological mother; my training in middle and high school; my specialized training program after; and now, basically being a contract for hire, serving all branches of the military providing independent criminal investigative, counterintelligence, and protective service outside the traditional military command. My assignments required me to proactively identify, investigate, and neutralize serious criminal, terrorist, and espionage threats. I figured that was enough to lay on him, so I didn't go into any details about my previous missions.

Tom poured himself another glass. He was deep in thought before he finally said, "So, essentially what you are telling me is...you're a badass."

"Well, I'd tell you more, but I'd have to kill you." He chuckled at that, but it was a little more nervous than natural.

"Tom, I wasn't looking for you, but here we are. Fate, or whatever you want to call it. I've spent my whole life, up to now, knowing what I wanted to do, and for the first time, ever, I feel vulnerable and it's not something I'm familiar with."

"Why didn't you just tell me?"

"Well, let's play this through. We had a chance encounter in which I was on a working assignment. How was I certain, at the time, that it was chance? Even after I was sure, how was I going to bring it up? 'Oh, by the way, I'm staying here to investigate a high-level threat, under suspicion of trafficking information of potentially global destruction.' I'm sure that would have gone over smoothly."

"What changed? Why are you telling me now?"

"Because...I can live without you...but I'm choosing not to."

"What took you so long?" He stated, more than asked.

Tada. And that's all she wrote, folks. Defining moments. It changed our direction, and today it changed my life, for the better.

And, as luck has it, just then my pager went off. Mother...

Being a hired contractor had perks and disadvantages. When we were contacted for an assignment, be it pager, call, note, or whatever, it was classical conditioning. It was the learning procedure in which a biologically potent stimulus (i.e. neutralize bad guys) was paired with a previously neutral stimulus (pager, call) which elicited a response (heightened awareness to eliminate threat).

Pavlov's dog. Not sure if that was a good thing or a bad thing. I had to call in.

Only two people knew how to contact me. Freddy and Bethany. This wasn't Bethany, so it was safe to assume I was cleared for the next assignment. I called in, and was simply instructed to be ready to depart in 24 hours and would get details then.

I walked back to Tom, who had wandered outside while I was calling in. He was more relaxed, legs stretched out, with hands behind his head. He watched me as I walked over, taking me in visually. He looked at me with ease. "You have to go, don't you?"

"I do, but not right this moment. I have some time. Are you sure this is what you want to sign on to?"

"If it means being with you, then I'm all on board. We'll figure it out. Just don't ever leave me with a goodbye note again. I can't handle that."

"I can promise you that. Come with me. I'd like to make up for that now."

Chapter 12
Jet Lag

Twenty-four hours later, I was packed and ready to go. Destination: Berlin, Germany, where I was to gather information and confirm and neutralize (if necessary) a Russian politician who was attending a summit and was threatening to expose top CIA operatives, which would compromise several missions and directives involving weapons of mass destruction.

I was going solo and was advised to pack my little black dress. Great, another horny MF. Probably best not to share this tidbit with Tom.

I wasn't flying private this go-around and made a mental note going forward that I needed to negotiate different terms for future projects. Being the newbie in the ranks, I relied on Freddy to commandeer many of these arrangements, but if it meant 15+ hours on a commercial flight, they could find someone else locally.

I was sardined in on an American flight with a quick stop in LHR. It was first class, but still the stench of sickness was in the air. People and kids hacking all over. *Cover your damn mouths.* Although I was on hiatus for 3 weeks, I felt lethargic as I embarked on the plane. I couldn't remember the last time I ever felt sick.

I got in my seat and promptly fell asleep for almost the full duration of the flight. Yikes, I didn't feel much better when I awoke, which was not like me at all. I administered myself a steroid shot in the bathroom before I got off, hoping to ward off anything while I was here. Thank God for my travel bag that had anything and everything you can think of.

Target located. Ivan Karpov. Summit was in 2 days.

My mission was to ensure he didn't make it to the summit. Until we knew for certain what he knew and didn't know, we couldn't afford for him to share any information with other nations. Easy peasy.

I located him roughly 2 miles away from The Ritz at Tausend, a confined, subtly lit bar with live music and Asian-American cuisine. He was sitting at the bar sipping on what appeared to be a Moscow Mule. The seat next to him was open. Lucky me.

I slid in next to him. I asked for a menu and eventually told the bartender that I'd have whatever the gentleman next to me was drinking, as I just couldn't make up my mind. The Asian smell in the restaurant was making me nauseous. WTF?!

Ivan was not an attractive man. Short, mid-fifties, and balding, with misplaced patches of hair, and a belly the size of Buddha. He looked like a fat John Malkovich. He had a mole the size of Berlin on the left side of his nose, which must have been Photoshopped out in the pics I had of him. Made it hard not to stare at it. Going with serious acting to make this credible. Based on his looks, I had already decided to go dirty blonde bob with hazel eyes. Even hookers would have a hard time with this creep, as there just wasn't enough money. Luckily for me, I wasn't sleeping with him, and despite the sub par commercial flying accommodations, they were paying me handsomely.

I was staying at The Ritz, where he was staying, so that helped offset the flight.

My drink couldn't come fast enough. Ivan was happy to have anyone sit next to him and was quite the chatty chap. Unfortunately, the open seat was on the side of the mole. When he laughed, the long hairs on his mole moved. My stomach churned. I wanted so badly to reach over and just pluck them from his fat head.

I introduced myself as Felicia Thomas, an executive admin here to attend the summit with my boss, a politician from Washington. That got the convo going.

The first Moscow Mule was settling on my stomach. God, I hope I didn't have the flu. No time for this. Ivan took the liberty and ordered another round as he talked about himself for the next 30 minutes. I tried to look amused as he talked, all the while imagining it would just be easier to put a bullet in his head and be done with it. When the second drink came, I was starting to sweat. Good grief, some damn screaming sick kid on that plane probably got me sick. We continued talking and I noticed a medical alert bracelet on Ivan, indicating penicillin. Good to know, that wasn't in his file.

I told Ivan that I had to leave to go meet my boss, but would love to meet him tomorrow at the same time if he was available. His dull, lifeless old eyes perked up as he excitedly said yes. I hugged him on his right side, trying to get the visual out of my mind. He was ordering another round as I departed.

I headed to The Ritz knowing that I had less than an hour to gather what I could from his room. The brisk night air was a relief, and I didn't feel nauseous any more. Probably just food poisoning. I made a quick stop first to my room. Getting into his room was not an issue. I called up for additional towels for the room beside his. When the bellhop came up, I fidgeted with Ivan's door and complained that these cheap new magnetic keys weren't working, and voila: he opened the door for me.

Once inside, I quickly maneuvered through all his items. His computer was up—no password, no login, nothing even encrypted. What a fool. Checked browser history and he was definitely a perv. Not sure the pedophile level, but he certainly liked them young. For their sakes, hopefully they were blind. Copied over everything he had and found the files I was looking for. Ol' Ivan had been a busy boy. He had documentation on three of the leadership team with the Director and two deputies for collusion with Russia and China. Looked like the intel he had was substantial but could be discredited by US as simply allegations.

He must be preparing to make this information public at the summit. Even if they couldn't prove it, it put top administration in bad light with too many eyes on their activities, which suspended other necessary tasks at hand. Perception was reality. I knew what I needed to do and headed to the bathroom.

I was in and out within 35 minutes and made my way down to the Curtain Club, a wonderfully elegant, uncommon bar in the Ritz. I hoped Ivan would pop in here on his way home, and as luck would have it, he strolled in

20 minutes after I arrived, already three sheets to the wind. He was excited that I was there. I explained that my boss left to finish up with some contract negotiations. He ordered drinks and I suggested we take them back to his room. He was more than willing to oblige. He must have been smoking cigars, as he reeked to high heaven when he talked. The nausea feeling was returning.

Upon entering his room, he was quick to try to get touchy. His mole hairs were giving me the heebie jeebies. I encouraged him to brush his teeth, since he'd been smoking, so I could get more comfortable. He practically ran to the bathroom to accommodate. He came back into the bedroom, smiling like an idiot. He started to grab a water, but I quickly got up to snatch it from his hand and sipped on it slowly, dripping some down my chest. He was unsuccessfully trying to take his pants off, now. Yikes, that wasn't pretty, either. I needed 20 more seconds.

He plopped on the bed and motioned for me to come join him and help him take his pants off. I eyed him and slowly made my way, taking as much time as I could. 3.2.1. and finally, it kicked in. His tongue started to get thick and then his eyes protruded. A shortness of breath engulfed his airwaves, now turning to full panic mode. He wobbled up with hands around his neck, trying to get to his briefcase. I didn't move. Didn't try to help. Just watched him. He poured everything out of his briefcase, freaking out, incredulous that he couldn't find what he was looking for. He was coughing and wheezing, with hives appearing on his face. He searched his bathroom and clothing. Nothing.

His eyes were streaked red and he was dizzy. He looked at me, begging. I looked at him and held up his Epipen for him to see, while he heard these final words, "At least your wife won't have to look at the fucking ugly mole again." His eyes bludgeoned with fear. He landed on the ground because of anaphylaxis. He wouldn't be making it to the summit.

When room service came in tomorrow, they'd find that Ivan died of a severe allergic reaction. They'd check, but not thoroughly, as nothing was taken or foul play suspected. They wouldn't know that files were missing or browsers cleared. His Epipen tragically was empty, lying by his side. They'd see his receipts for too many drinks, and would write it off that he must have come in contact with something, but was too drunk to administer his antidote in time. They'd never suspect his toothpaste, where penicillin was injected.

Two hours later I was on a flight headed back to LAX. I sat in first class, exhausted. Figured it was just a combination of jet lag, probable food poisoning, and physical exhaustion. I fell asleep upon takeoff and awoke an hour later with my eyes wide open in panic.

There was another possibility I hadn't even considered.

Chapter 13
Awakening

I told Tom that I would head to his house upon my arrival. I had the driver stop off at a store, first. Tom was excited to see me, and I was, too, albeit a little tired. I excused myself quickly to freshen up in the bathroom and took a quick shower. I came out with a towel on my head with one of his robes on and joined him in the kitchen where he was making something to snack on.

We chatted about the assignment, and I told him the bits and pieces that I thought were necessary and relevant. We had already discussed a hard rule of what I could and couldn't, or shouldn't, divulge. He understood it was for his protection, too.

As we sat at his breakfast table, he reached over to my hand and said, "I have something I want to share with you."

Yikes, me too. I looked at him and said, "Before you do, there's something I should share with you, first." Deep breath in, deep breath out.

I was soaking in his relaxed look, and how perfect he was for me on so many levels. This was going to change everything, if not ruin it. I could feel my chest beating, going in and out.

"Matti, are you going to tell me or make me guess?" he said, smiling.

3.2.1. – I reached into the robe pocket and took out a stick and placed it in front of him on the table, face down. His eyes got wide with shock or anticipation. He slowly picked it up and turned it over. Just one simple marking on it: it was a blue + sign.

He got up from the table and moved over to me, grasped my face, and gave me a kiss, followed by a big smile. My eyes showed the expressions I was feeling, from grateful, anxious, and nervous, to fearful. He bent down on one knee, held my hands together, and said, "Well, the timing for what I need to share is just perfect." With that, he grabbed into his pants pocket and pulled out a ring.

I hadn't expected this. My thoughts were reeling. I didn't even know what to say. We hadn't spent much time together, but it just felt right.

Before I could get anything out, he started with this: "Matti, I'm sure you think this is crazy. We haven't even known each other long. But I know you. I also know that I don't want to live without you. You are everything I could ever ask for; you are witty, smart, intelligent, confident, and obviously messed up, with the line of work you are in, but that's attractive, too."

Here he was before me...kind, gentle, funny, educated, gainfully employed, and gorgeous, presenting me with a brilliant band with pave diamonds with a center round bordered in a French-set halo. Never thought I'd like a round diamond, but big round looked pretty damn sweet. I must be crazy or hormonal already.

I sat there looking at this ring. I never envisioned myself being married. After all, who was I going to find that accepted me for who I am? Did I find him out of blind luck? Would this change me and everything I worked so hard for? I couldn't let it.

It felt like seconds, but must have been longer, as he was watching me patiently, then finally broke in with: "Well, I was hoping you'd be a little bit more excited or at least respond with a yes, by now."

I just looked at him and smirked. "Sorry, babe, I was trying to figure out who to call first."

Relief flooded over him and he picked me up and carried me into the bedroom. The good news: I couldn't get pregnant again.

We lay in bed after, laughing at how crazy this all was. Neither of us wanted a big wedding. He didn't have any family and I couldn't afford to bring attention to me with my work, so going to the Justice of the Peace it would be. Neither of us wanted to wait. Of course, I had to bring in some logistics. Like how my work would always be a priority to me, and it would dictate how and where we lived, at times. And now, we were going to do this with a child. With him franchising his business, we would have opportunities to move, if necessary. We both were financially doing very well, so we had means, and now we had each other. Good grief, getting sappy.

I lay on my side and just stared at him. He really was perfect. And he was mine.

I had three calls to make, and wasn't sure which one I wanted to make first. I had Mom/Dad, and Bethany and Freddy. I wasn't looking forward to calling Freddy. I got ahold of Mom, first. Dad was at the campus. Started with informal chit chat, just catching up. I asked her if she was sitting down as I had some news to share. I then laid on her that I was pregnant and was going to get married at a local Justice of the Peace. She was happy, but I think possibly reflective, thinking back to her sister and how her world would have changed had she done or had the ability to do what I'm doing. I'm sure she was conflicted with her emotions, but she seemed generally happy for me and us. I told her to apologize to Dad that I couldn't tell him at the same time, but that I'd try to get back to see them soon.

Bethany flipped her shit when I told her. She was excited, but surprised and mad as hell, as she thought I was holding back on her. Told her that could never be the case, as she was my Day 1 and would always be. She inquired how I was going to tell Freddy. I'm not sure why I had such trepidation for a man I have never physically met, but the anxiety was real. Told her I wasn't sure, but that was my next call. Bethany hung up with "Good luck with that." Yikes.

Better to just get it over with. I dialed Freddy, hoping I'd get voicemail and could delay this, but no such luck. He answered on the second ring. He started right in on Ivan and asked if I could just leave once without making a mess. I took offense, naturally.

"Let me get this straight. You sent me, in your words, to confirm and neutralize a situation. I confirmed he had damning information that would jeopardize multiple missions and the US. I confirmed he was a perv. I neutralized the situation. Sorry, my bad: I just assumed you wanted to tell me 'thank you' or something like that."

"That wasn't what I meant. I just wished you would reach out before you take matters into your own hands."

"Not to steal a line from *Top Gun* again, but 'You don't have time to think.'""

Freddy was quick with his retort: "I think the line is...*The enemy's dangerous, but right now you're worse. Dangerous and foolish.*"

"Wow. You're right. I think the line I should have started with is, *"What's your problem?"*

With that, Freddy eased off momentarily and then asked me to brief him in more detail. After I finished, he agreed that my options were limited and the outcome the most likely best conclusion. So, again, my point was...you're welcome.

Deep breath in. Deep breath out.

"Freddy, this isn't the reason why I was actually calling." I decided just to get straight to the point. "Remember when you asked if there was going to be any blowback from my...um... companionship?"

"Oh God, please don't tell me you offed him, too."

Slight nervous chuckle. "Well, um no; it took a different turn. We're pregnant and getting married."

Nothing. Not a word. Complete silence.

"You there?" I asked after a long awkward pause.

"I'm here. I'm vacillating on what to say. Do I start with congratulations, or do you realize you've just thrown all your training and dedication out the window for a stranger?"

Boy, he sure could get on my nerves quickly.

"Well, I didn't think this was going to go smoothly, but I'll take the congratulations first and throw in for you, since you don't seem to have the capability: 'I'm really happy for you'," I retorted.

"It's not like you gave me a lot of lead time on this, Matti. If this is what you want, go for it. I just think you are limiting your future on a whim."

"You underestimate me, Freddy. I can have what you haven't accomplished, having both a personal and professional life, and despite what you think, I will continue to succeed in my work. I'm not being naïve. I know what this does and how it changes things, but it doesn't change the fundamentals of who I am."

"For your sake, I hope you can, Matti. And despite what you think you know, I understand the complexities of it more intimately than you will ever know."

WTF did that mean?

"We good, Freddy?"

"We're good, Matti."

With that, he changed topic and mentioned that Bethany was being deployed locally and that I needed to be ready in the event she needed additional backup. He filled me in on some other work-related items and wrapped it up with saying he'd be in touch.

Before he hung up, I interjected. "Freddy, I know I caught you off guard today. I am sorry. I hadn't planned this, and that's not like me, so this is new territory for me, too. As crazy and illogical it may seem, I know it's the right thing for me. You knew my mother, and I think she would be happy for me right now, and glad I'm choosing this direction. I promise I'm committed to my work and I'm not leaving you. I'll try not to throw in too many surprises going forward."

"Kiddo, she would be happy; and given time, I will be, too. Try not to throw me for any more loops so I can recover, will ya?"

"Look at you, you old softie. Talk soon, Freddy." And I hung up.

All seemed to be going well and I assisted on some local projects. A few weeks later, Tom and I went for our first sonogram, where our world would be rocked again.

We weren't having one, but THREE babies. The only thought going through my head, was: shit, how was I going to tell Freddy this?

Chapter 14
Trifecta

The thing with being young is you don't know what you don't know. I thought I was invincible. I was educated, trained...hell, I was widely known and recognized in a small circle of select contractors. Tom was great. We were great. His work was flourishing and he was a doting husband. We married at the ol' Justice of Peace, with just Bethany as our witness. We returned home where Tom had John Michael Montgomery playing...*You are the love of my life...strong and wild...*

Tom was the perfect man. I told him I'd picked out a song for us too, and turned on Garth Brooks' *"Shameless"* and serenaded him with my horrible tone-deaf singing...*Well I'm shameless...*

It was a perfect night.

My pregnancy was going as smoothly as one could hope. Where I struggled was between work and my identity. I continued operations up until my fourth month, but once I started showing, my options were limited. All the while, Bethany was being assigned some fantastic missions and was really excelling. I was happy for her, but at the same time felt conflicted. My job was ingrained with who I was, and I felt like I was missing out. I was envious. What did I expect? Naïve.

It was turbulent times in terms of national security. Between nuclear weapons of mass destruction, Sadam Hussein, Ayatollah Khomeini, and even the deceased Pablo Escobar, the list went on. Religion, drugs, greed – all equal wars. So much was not addressed with the public based on the frenzied pandemonium that would ensue. With technological advances, we now had access to more real-time information that it took whole teams to decipher. I was in these back lines now, deciphering what, where, and who; and directing others for the next tasks. The good part was that I was tied in with multiple branches, be it Seals, Rangers, MI6, and others. Interesting fact: Seal Team Six was named that to confuse the Soviets, as we were only operating two teams, at the time. Perception versus reality. It was hard to navigate to the truth.

By the end of August, I was twenty-five weeks into my pregnancy and going through a whirlwind of emotions. Things were too quiet on the home front, which made me nervous. Momma Bear instinctive mode was on heightened alert. I felt like I was missing vital information and was now going manic at work, combing through every bit of information. Tom assumed it was just pregnancy hormones, but I felt there was more. Freddy had been distant ever since, but he too felt like something was coming. There were too many signals that no one was paying attention to. The CIA, FBI, and the military were always looking for the obvious, but to truly understand our enemies, you must think like them; not hope they act like us. It was a continual mistake we made. Can you recognize the difference between evil, brilliance, or just sheer determination? With nuclear weapons on heightened alert, everyone was looking for large items. All the cross chatter we were ferreting through made me think this was another rope-a-dope; that they were wanting us to be misled so we would miss the obvious signals.

I remember vividly when I called Freddy in a panic. It was September 10th. I told him something was going down and I needed to bump my clearance, as I knew there was additional information that was being suppressed. I laid out all the information I had and Freddy agreed that he thought we needed to move this up the chain. We talked through plausible situations and conclusions. I kept reiterating that we had to stop thinking about how someone brought something in and more about what they would use that they already had access to. Dates, times, and locations: we poured over each scenario and continued to come up short. By the end of the call, Freddy knew we were onto something and said he'd handle it so we could get access, and he told me to just try and get some rest. He respected that I was committed to my work and I had not been deterred simply because I was pregnant.

At midnight on September 11th, I awoke doubled over. I woke Tom and told him something was wrong; we needed to get to the hospital now. We raced there to learn that baby #1 had his hand sticking out and was bringing the other two with him. A foreboding presence was all around and I knew Tom was worried not that he would lose just his babies, but his new wife, too. They called in a specialist, as there was no time for an epidural. Trust me, I wanted the drugs.

Tom was holding my hand when I told him I needed to call Freddy. He was baffled as to why I wanted to call him now and said we could wait till after the kids were born. I looked at Tom and said, "I know what they are going to do. It will be a random act, and it will cause us to have daily fear, and that will paralyze our economy because of it."

After that, I doubled over on the bed and the doctors took me back to do an emergency C-section.

I awoke to Tom holding my hand. He was tired, but smiling. He said we had three healthy babies, albeit premature by almost 3 months—two boys and one girl. All were small, weighing in at 2 pounds each, but all healthy. They just needed to feed and grow. My heart swelled, it was so full.

Tom took my hand and said, "I have something else to tell you. The doctors wanted me to wait, but I know you'll want to know immediately." I had an instant panic, worrying that one of the kids was missing a body part and was deformed or worse. He saw my face and instantly comforted me and said it was nothing to do with the kids. Relieved, I then worried about my parents, Bethany, and Freddy. Again, Tom assured me, and I finally said just get to it.

"Babe, your instincts were right. The timing was just off. The US was attacked today by random airplanes hitting the twin towers, the Pentagon, and a town in Pennsylvania. The casualties are over 3,000 at best guess, right now. The President has declared there will be retribution."

"Please turn on the TV, and bring me my phone."

I watched the furor for the next hour, catching up on every newsfeed; processing every detail that I could. I watched people falling or jumping to their deaths from the burning towers; firefighters and workers losing their own lives. Surreal to think it happened whilst I was delivering new life into this world. My blood boiled.

The nurses came in and said I could be wheeled down to see my babies. I watched as these tiny hands and feet clung to life. Tubes came out all over, things helped them breathe, but I watched as each one took a breath in and a breath out. I looked at all the other babies in the NICU, with organs on wrong side or missing limbs, and knew how blessed and fortunate we were. I heard what I thought was a baby wailing, waiting for the nurse to go over and caress it, only to see it was a grieving mother who just lost her newborn child.

Coming from my religious background, we went with traditional Catholic names: Mathew, Mark and Mary.

I took out my phone and called Freddy. Tom had called him when they took me back. Tom must have been scared to death to do so. Freddy asked how I was and I filled him in on seeing the kids. We quickly went to the current events and he simply said, "Your hunch was right. NSA had intercepted a call about this a while back and didn't think anything nefarious would come of it. The CIA had been alerted as well, but didn't share this with the FBI, State, or Justice Departments. It was a simple case of one hand not knowing what the other was doing. I got access late last night and by the time I caught a thread, the acts were already occurring. There was no time to stop it."

"You know what this means, Freddy?"

"I'm afraid so," he said.

"Game on, motherfuckers. I'm just getting started. No Man Left Behind."

Chapter 15
Time Warp

Kids were a time suck. (I should have been in *Rocky Horror Picture Show* singing that *Time warp* song...*Madness takes its toll...You're into a time slip...And nothing can ever be the same...*)

You can read all those parenting books you want, but don't waste your time. They never tell you the true issues you need concern yourself with, like, #1 - sleep deprivation. Tom and I were so sleep deprived those first 6 months, we barely recalled anything. The first three months they were in NICU just growing and feeding, but requiring "kangaroo," which is to lay them on your bare skin so they can hear and feel you breathing. Oh, and you can't talk, since you are in there with other babies. You're supposed to do this at least two times a day for 3 hours each time. Now, times that by 3 kids. Do that math. WTF! I did mainly the day shift while Tom did night, while each of us tried to squeeze in work after we were done with our shifts. Once the kids were home, they were only 5 pounds each, so they were on a 2.5- to 3-hour schedule, but now we didn't have nurses to help us. I was militant on keeping the kids on a routine; otherwise, we would never be able to sleep. Tom didn't have family or close friends to help. My mom came when she could, but had to get back to her own world; Bethany was out on missions; and I had no other friends, either. We had a Starbucks nearby and they had our drinks ready at 6AM every morning as these kids woke up at 4:30AM on the dot. I thought they were possessed.

September 11th, my kids' birth date, would forever be remembered as the coordinated terrorist attacks by Al-Qaeda resulting in 2,977 people murdered, over 6,000 injured, and causing billions in infrastructure and property damage, not including the effect on global markets. The Department of Homeland Security and the USA Patriot Act were created to detect and prosecute terrorism and hate crimes. NSA was given more power with warrantless surveillance. Britain stood beside the US.

Only one month after the attacks, Bush launched the War on Terror to depose the Taliban with aerial bombings targeting the Taliban and Al-Qaeda, along with ground troops and Special Forces invading Afghanistan. My colleagues were dying fighting for our country and I was dealing with croup at home. The kids alone were enough to give someone a mental breakdown, but I had lived my life and trained for this and felt utterly helpless. It was breaking my will.

Six months after giving birth, I had a knock on the door. It would change our lives. My first thought was, "Who the hell is knocking on the damn door? Can't you read the sign 'Do NOT knock. Babies SLEEPING'? I opened the door to a familiar face; one that made me beam from ear to ear.

"I heard you may need some help," she said with a Southern drawl.

"God, I've missed you!" I said as I hugged her, and had tears in my eyes. I didn't want to let go.

It was like an angel knew what I needed and sent Miss Peterson in for the rescue. Come to find out it wasn't divine in nature, but Freddy, who came to my rescue once again.

And, just like that, my course and direction was changed. Now in her fifties, she was still the sharpest person I knew. Not only could she train and educate, but she had wisdom beyond her years. She loved kids and I knew she would protect mine as her own. She continued to give her life to help others serve, and was now here to help me. My will was restored. It was time to re-engage...completely.

I called Freddy.

"Hey, I got two things for you," I said matter-of-factly when he answered.

"Shoot," he replied.

"One, thanks. Two, I'm back."

"You're welcome, and about time."

I think Tom was even happier than I was. Rule #2 on kids; you can never be fully prepared. Maybe that should be moved to rule #1. We went out to our first meeting place, Chateau Marmont, to celebrate and discuss what this meant for our future. Tom fully embraced and supported me in my cause and missions. Secretly, I think part of him wanted to be included. His main concern now was the balance aspect, as he knew I had a (strong) tendency to be OCD.

Tom was doing great with his business and was already franchising. This provided us opportunity and more resources to move, if necessary. Miss Peterson (or Tia, as we now referred to her) would assist us in the care and upbringing of our children. I would continue (to outsiders) with my rouse of being an airline stewardess, and this allowed me to leave on missions with plausible reason. I promised never to be away more than 10 days at a time, and this proved occasionally cumbersome with undercover missions abroad. I attempted to select more North/South America missions, of which we had plenty of opportunities between drugs and immigration.

Time warp.

Fourteen years flew by in the blink of an eye.

The triplets are as different as can be. I still grimace when people ask me if they are identical. People really are f'in stupid. Even when I explain it would be difficult, since one is a female...you can still see the blank stare as they try to compute. God help this country. Each kid had a natural ability that Miss Peterson developed and honed. All were good kids and were good-looking. Not biased; just stating facts.

Matthew is slender and muscular and excels in cross-country and history in school. Out of the three, he is most inclined to follow in Mom's footsteps. I see him going into strategic warfare. He is a deep thinker, and is kind to others while being witty. His specialty leans towards guns and explosives and he is fluent in languages.

Mary needed no guidance from the beginning. She is her mother's child, but is even smarter and better-looking. She is driven and self-reliant. She started writing code early and enjoys technology. At school, she is a cheerleader and is the president of multiple clubs. Miss Peterson developed her skills in knives and biological warfare, and would most likely be running her own company(s). She also had expensive tastes. She got that trait from her Dad.

Mark is his father's spitting image. He is the tallest of the three, and likes to playfully remind the others that he was the last child delivered. He is charismatic, playful, and likes the ladies. He plays football and runs track, while learning early how to maneuver any type of machinery. Being our only lefty in the family, he is ambidextrous, which helps him to excel in most sports, and he will most likely take over his family business when it's time (or, if he had his druthers, he'll be a male model. There's always one in each family, what can I say?).

The kids know what I do for a living, to a degree, and understand the importance. Just as I've done with Tom, I don't go into details, but it's hard to miss when Mom comes home with bruises or contusions. I cover as well as I can, and usually steer them into thinking I'm doing more reconnaissance work than anything else. After repeatedly watching The Wiggles and every Disney movie when the kids were younger, I found myself wanting to do more fieldwork as I caught myself singing *"Hot Potato, Hot Potato,"* or crying when the princess lost her mother. (Talk about some messed-up people when every Disney movie doesn't have a mother in it. Someone has some serious issues). I worry that my kids will never be normal, as my boys have been brought up by a masculine female and I never could braid my daughter's hair. She can throw a mean spiral, though, so I guess there's that trade-off.

Tom, the natural salesman, loves conversing with others and is successfully franchising his business across the US. We are partners, lovers, and best friends and have a great work/life balance between our two professions. Our only differences and arguments lie in our TV watching. On the rare occasions when we do watch TV, it's football, or he likes *The Bachelor*. It drives me crazy on both fronts. Every time they bring out the chains in the NFL, I go crazy, as it's such a crapshoot, and with technology, surely there is a better way to measure. I continue to argue that there is some truth that championships can be rigged not like Bruce Willis in *The Last Boy Scout,* but more like *The Natural.* In terms of *The Bachelor*, I must admit that Tom has a feminine side that I don't possess. I call him 'Nancy' when he watches. I'm not sure if he borders on hopeless romantic or deranged fool. He loves being on the outside of my work, and has been very helpful with his psychology Masters knowledge that I've applied to some of my tougher interrogations. I became even more proficient in my manipulations with targets, while staying in control, because of his guidance.

We had Bethany become Tom's operational manager, which allowed her to be connected to us and provided cover for our travel. It was the perfect set-up. Her choices in men continue to baffle us, as she could pick a loser out of any crowd. Still not married, her former lovers are either dead, in prison, or missing teeth. Have to give her credit: she is a lover of life and goes with the flow and is still the funniest person I know. We work out and continue to PR in many areas, even as we age, and she still kicks my ass at times, and I remind her it was because hers is still bigger. She and I have taken a few physical hits because of our profession, and can thank some good docs for fixing us back up. That sick fuck Miquel set me back in Positano; otherwise, my KDR (Kill to Death Ratio) is on my side. Bethany and I are at the range consistently, working on our American Sniper status.

We moved three times during these 14 years as a security measure to ensure that my cover was not exposed. From LA, we went to DC, then Atlanta, followed by Chicago, which coincided with new franchise openings. From tracking down weapons of mass destruction, insurgents, immigration, cartels, and child endangerment to dealing with changes in presidential administrations, I continued my quest for US security. The threats are real and ever-evolving and the public will never know about or understand how it all intertwines and threatens our very existence, daily. I wish I could be as ignorant, at times.

While serving my country, I have had to balance with the kids' lives, and attempted to plug myself into community and school organizations to blend in and assist with my cover. I found this trying, to say the least. From divorced parents arguing over who was listed first in the directory (they are in fucking kindergarten, people), to campaigning for top positions in the talent show (it's a fucking hula hoop skit), to neighborhood squabbles over the color of the mailbox (if it should be black or matte black—good grief), I understand why some people are medicated (or should be). Tom and I made a few close friends, but only surface level, because of my line of work and our travels.

Although Freddy and I talk every day, I've still never met him in person, and this frustrates me to the core. Although I'm superb at tracking, he is even better and continues to elude my searches. I consistently ask him why, and he always responds that it's just better this way.

Freddy and I argue repeatedly on approaches. Since we are outside contractors, our influence in governmental offices is limited, despite being successful on our missions. A big flaw in our ideology, to me, is that we continue to operate with countries/individuals whom we expect to respond rationally. Our enemies do not operate this way, and history will repeat if we do not adjust our way of thinking. Suicide bombers are a perfect example. How do you rationalize that? This is not about targeting a specific color or race. We are trained not to stereotype.

Time warp. It was now 2015, and Freddy was sending me to Kabul. Mother f'er. I was going to have to go Charlize Theron ala *Mad Max* mode. My special effects makeup techniques for disguise were on point, and I chose to go Kim Kardashian meets Sally Field in *Not Without My Daughter* vibe. Sexy Sally with a Hijab. Yeah, that should do it.

Chapter 16
FUBAR

When we sent troops to Afghanistan, once we deployed them, we had to win at all costs. President Bush and Obama promised to bring troops back, but we could not afford to lose over there once we entered. If we lost, the ideology would allow them to enter the US with aspirations for redemption and repetition. We would have to stay over there permanently at an extreme cost, both financially and in lives lost.

Kabul is the capital of Afghanistan, grew from 500,000 to over 4 million by time US troops invaded, and was a strategic location along trade routes, with 18 districts. There was war against armies here and war against people: international terrorist groups, suicide bombers, and the senseless rape and killing of all people. Some considered it ethnic cleansing. US troops traveled by helicopters for a 5-mile jaunt for fear of retaliation by the people we were helping. How was that for thanks? We started striking Taliban leaders as our means to end this via air strikes and drone attacks. Taliban commanders were changing almost monthly, but the insurgents were just as powerful and determined and were uprising. Their motto was that Americans would pay for the murders of their family, children, and friends.

My mission was simple. Locate and neutralize a potential upcoming commander. Easy peasy. With suicide bombers on buses and railways and in coffee houses, the most concerning part of plotting this mission turned out to be on traveling with the unknown and the self-righteous. Our government couldn't afford to send special ops in to get notoriety from this mission. The Deputy Director requested me. In a male dominated field, my record spoke for itself. This wasn't a sanctioned mission.

I was going to have to break my pact with Tom, as this was going to be longer in duration than normal—I estimated a minimum of three weeks. The kids had a break coming up, so the timing was good and hopefully that would be a good diversion. Before any mission, Tom and I always took time to ourselves—not for a doomsday preparation, but that was always the unspoken thought. We discussed kids' schedules, communication, best case versus worst case scenarios, timing, and the ultimate GTFO (or Get the Fuck Out) scenario. Each time, we would end the evening with a bottle of Abacus. Why not?

Something most have felt foreboding, because on this night, I suggested we open another. Tom surprised me with a simple gift of an 18K gold, slender, dainty choker chain with a barely visible "Mama" inscribed in cursive in the middle. I looked at this man, incredulous at how lucky I was to find him and the life we had. I grabbed his hand and led him back to the bedroom where I told him I'd have to show him my gift.

The next day, packed and ready, I hugged all the kids and Tom longer than usual and told them I'd be with them as soon as I could. Tom looked at me, and the first and only time he had ever said anything before deployment, he said, "I don't have a good feeling about this trip." I didn't, either, and I didn't know why. I looked at him and tried to reassure him with, "You don't need to worry about me, baby. I got this."

I headed to O'Hare, and with much reluctance, flew commercial on Emirates. Flying private was too risky and I didn't want to bring any undue attention to myself. I had 22 hours on the flight to sleep and prep, as I planned to hit the ground running. I had a contact on the ground who had set up a residence for me and would aid in other logistics—namely weapons—and be my driver. Flying in disguise, I was now Aamirah Asadi. Aamirah stood for a woman inhabiting a place (which was true) and Asadi, meaning to love freedom (also true). I enjoyed the irony, what can I say.

I was looking for a Mohammad Omari Aktar. Mohammad = Praise, Omari = Flourishing, Aktar = a Star. I wasn't going to be praising any flourishing star, but was instructed to diminish it. Oh, and we couldn't confirm Aktar's identity, so that added to the complexity of the mission.

Per the Global Terrorism Database, over the last 40 years, 75 percent of terrorist attacks took place in 10 countries: Iraq, Afghanistan, India, the Philippines, Somalia, Turkey, Nigeria, Yemen and Syria. Military, special ops, and contractors were trained not to be racially persuaded, but targeted those countries to stop acts aimed at attaining a political, economic, religious or social goal that inflicted death on others in an effort to influence policy. We called these people violent extremists, and they came in all color and creeds. Despite intense media attention, though, terrorist acts leading to death were still a relatively low number compared to other violent deaths, especially in the US. The devastation terrorism could cause to our economy was not relative, thus this was why we were sent to friendly and unfriendly nations alike to help spearhead efforts to contain or eliminate threats.

I forced myself to sleep now, knowing the conditions that I'd be entering. I left my ear buds in and woke up to Bush, *Machinehead* lyrics...*Breathe in...breath out...*

I opened my eyes and we landed. Upon my arrival, I met my contact, Fareed. 'Fareed' meant unique or alone, and was quite fitting for him, as well. Roughly 5'8, with black hair and dark brown eyes, he was about the same height and weight as me. Raised in the US as Chris Webb, he returned to his parents' native country in his twenties and had been working undercover for the US since. He had been instrumental in locating key targets and assisting in outside operations. As I arrived in the baggage area, Fareed was there, and greeted me with a customary hand over the chest, saying "Salam alaikum" (meaning 'Hello'). I greeted him with a handshake to indicate family or a close personal friend. Every culture had rules for social behavior, and this was certainly true in Afghanistan.

Once inside his private vehicle, only then did he look at me in the eyes from his rearview mirror and ask how my trip was. I instantly liked him after only conversing with him for a few minutes. The magnitude was not lost on me, of the risks he was taking on this mission. Not just for me, but for the US. Naturally, Freddy had orchestrated this arrangement.

Hamid International Airport is located between mountains and desert plains, less than 10 miles from the center of Kabul. The US also happened to bomb it after 9/11, and in 2008 the North Side Cantonment was turned over to the US Armed Forces. As Fareed maneuvered outside the airport, heading to the denser population and terrain of the mountains, we conversed about the logistics of the mission.

Less than 15 minutes into the ride, Fareed looked back at me in the rearview mirror and said, "Miss Matti, I think we may have a tail."

"That would be most unexpected, considering that only 3 people knew I was coming here, with you being one," I said calmly as my hands moved inside my wardrobe to the wiring of my bra, which contained a thin dart containing two lethal injection portals.

"I can assure you, it is not me," he said as he looked at me in the mirror, understanding the next move, if I had any doubt or hesitation.

Not wanting to bring attention to us yet, Fareed changed lanes, streets, and directions. Our tail was still present.

Fareed looked at me and asked, "What do you want to do?"

"What do you have access to in the car?" I responded.

"I carry a Smith & Wesson XVR460 Magnum."

"Nice; extra rounds?"

"No."

"Pass it all back and let's try to outrun them first, before we bring them in closer."

Had Fareed been involved, he would have had hesitated in passing back his weapon, or would have used it as his opportunity to eliminate me. He did neither, but passed it back earnestly. He would have to be an incredible actor if he was just biding time, at this point.

Now, increasing speed, Fareed's intimate knowledge of the city proved most beneficial, but to no avail. It was like a scene out of *Navy Seals* with Charlie Sheen and Michael Biehn, with two cars chasing within the winding roads. There was no chance of not hitting something or someone, at this point, and our main goal was not to end up at a dead-end, or dead. Fareed was outpacing them, at this point, but they were still in range and were now shooting with semi-automatics, with bullets racing by us. Good news: they weren't sharpshooters, but we wouldn't be able to keep this up.

I took out my burner phone. It was time to call for some outside help. I dialed Freddy.

"Hello, Ms. Baker, we were expecting your call," I heard the male voice say as he answered the phone.

WTF?! *Breathe in, Breathe out.* "I'm sorry, who do I have the pleasure of speaking with?"

"That's unimportant; what is of the utmost importance for your friend, here, is the location of something we have been looking for and which is in your personal possession."

Fuck you. "I have no idea to what you are referencing, so get to the point." Patience was not my virtue.

"We've been looking for you for quite some time, now. Seems like you have been well connected and well hidden. I believe your dead mother gave you something that belongs to us, and we want it back."

"Interesting. You've been looking for me for quite some time, then. Let me ask you something: would you rather be known as stupid, or inept? Oh hell, does it really matter?" With that, I hung up and told Fareed we were going to have to come up with Plan B.

I had no time. I texted Tom and Bethany together (GTFO, I love you.). I quickly dismantled the phone and threw the pieces out the window.

My mind raced, playing out the scenarios. The only reason for them to keep Freddy alive now was to get to me. He would be tortured first; there was no getting around that. He didn't know where I had the vials. He'd specifically told me never to tell him, just for this type of event.

They would need me alive. If they captured me, they would kill Freddy anyways. Most likely, that was going to happen, regardless. You couldn't reason with crazy. My heart ached momentarily as my mind calculated my next moves.

My thoughts immediately went to the Deputy Director, the only other person who knew my whereabouts and who had specifically requested me. Motherfucker. It was hard enough, but even worse when it was an inside job – the ultimate betrayal. If it was the last thing I did, I would watch him burn. It wasn't his voice, but it had to be one of his men.

The chance of outrunning the tail was minute. Unless they careened into a building, 5 rounds were all I had to deflect and target. We would need them to get closer. I told Fareed to slow down just a bit and let them catch up, and he naturally responded with: "You want me to do *what*?!" and I filled him in on the new plan.

There were four men in the black sedan. The plan was simple. Lure them closer into an area where we'd make sudden turn and stop, allowing us time to shoot out driver, front passenger and/or tires and hopefully take one more of those fuckers out in the process; all the while trying not to get hit ourselves. With only 5 rounds. Neither of us had knowledge of their background, training, or intent. That would require me to be a better aim than four men combined, and Fareed a better driver than them. The odds were slim, but the newer concern was that they had already called for backup.

Fareed knew an area to do this, and drove like Mario Andretti to get us there to get our plan in action, all the while with bullets careening past us. Just before slowing, he asked one last time if I was sure if this is what we wanted to do.

"Let's do this, Fareed; and before I forget, thank you in advance."

As Fareed was dodging dilapidated buildings and pot-holed streets, he pointed ahead to where we would be turning. He was buckled up for an oncoming collision, but I had to be free to face backwards to shoot. Lucky for me, they had already shot out the back window. I just hoped any impact wouldn't be significant. He slowed, then yanked a hard right turn and slowed down to a near stop.

You saw the white of their eyes as they became suddenly aware that we had stopped with no time for them to react. I aimed and shot the driver and passenger in the head, while the backseat passengers ducked for cover. I then shot out both front tires and yelled at Fareed to haul ass. As he sped up, I repositioned myself and glimpsed into the rearview mirror to see movement in the backseat as they took aim. They weren't playing games anymore as they lifted a RPG into position. So much for the theory that they wanted me alive, as these were designed to penetrate tank armor. RPGs were not guided towards targets by heat sensors or IR signatures, and couldn't be controlled in flight after launch. I yelled at Fareed to take a hard right.

We almost made it.

The next sixty seconds were slow motion and a blur. Fareed, at racing speeds, was attempting to yank a hard turn, causing the explosion of the RPG to just miss and detonate in front of us. The impact from the explosion forced our car to careen and slam into a building, rolling over before we landed upside down. Smoke billowed everywhere from the dusty streets and explosion. I couldn't see initially, and momentarily couldn't hear, due to the deafening boom. Disoriented and trying to gain my bearings, I knew I had sustained some serious injuries, as I was aware I wasn't even in the car anymore, but had been thrown from it. My eyes heavy, I touched my head and felt the blood oozing out. I knew I had to get that under control, but was trying to focus, first. As I tried to regain control, I looked for Fareed, who was slumped over the driver seat and who appeared to have taken the brunt of the explosion. He wasn't moving.

The ringing in my ears was deafening as I feebly attempted to prop myself up, to no avail. I saw the shadow of a man coming towards me. My mind told me to get up, but my body was unable to cooperate, just like Apollo Creed in *Rocky II*. I couldn't speak, but felt that I was yelling. Almost unconscious, I knew he was grabbing my hands and tying them together. I felt myself being dragged on the hot, rocky pavement before I totally blacked out from the pain.

I have no idea how much time passed before I woke up again. It could have been minutes, hours, or days. I was in a dimly-lit room. A kill room. It could have been straight out of *Casino Royale* with Daniel Craig, where they had him tied, naked, with his wrists behind a chair. My dark wig lay on the ground. I was tied to a workout bench, of all things, with only my bra and underwear on. I wondered why they left me with these on and grateful, as it could lead to their ultimate demise. I still had possession of the dart's two lethal doses. They left my feet untied, too, which would help me with balance. My head dangling down to my chest, I listened first, before I opened my eyes. I heard multiple men; one speaking in English, the others in Arabic. The American man dominated the conversation and you could sense the growing frustration of his concerns. They were arguing over next steps and exposure: that this could lead back to them.

I tried to listen more closely to sense if anyone had direct eyes on me— breathing, motion, anything—but I felt nothing but the searing pain in my head, throbbing, and I felt like my left side had been dragged down a burning volcano. Focus, damn it.

I slowly twitched my eyes to see if I could see anything in my peripheral vision. Nothing. I could make out that the men were in the other room behind a large glass window that looked into my area. Underneath me was large plastic cloth. They wanted to dispose of me afterwards without leaving a trace. I knew what was coming, and the powerlessness of it all. I thought of Tom and the kids and knew I wouldn't see them again. A single tear slid down my face. Fuck these bastards; they weren't getting anything from me. I just needed the right moment.

I lifted my head and looked around. The room was clear. My head felt like I had been beaten with a crowbar. Two doors led out of the room; one to the adjoining room that they were in and the other to who knew what, but it looked like an exterior door. I was in the middle of a 40x40 room. Nothing else was in there but the bench, me, and the plastic body tarp...and a set of pliers, knives, and a blowtorch lined up on the floor. Motherfuckers.

I looked at the window and said, "Let's get this going, you sick fucks. I don't have all day." The men were taken aback by my outburst and I saw them huddle as two of them headed towards me. The American stayed back. He was the ringleader and I made out that he was the US Deputy Director. Things just went from bad to worse.

I recalled an article we were obligated to read during our training. In 1955, The Office of Armed Forces published an article on The U.S. Fighting Man's Code. Then President

Dwight D. Eisenhower stated that *"every member of the Armed Forces of the US is expected to measure up to the standards embodied in this Code of Conduct while he is in combat or activity. To ensure achievement of these standards, each member of the Armed Forces liable to capture shall be provided with specific training and instruction designed to better quip him to counter withstand all enemy efforts against him and shall be fully instructed as to the behavior and obligations expected of him during combat or captivity."* I made a mental note that this lesson's material was seriously outdated and that I needed to send a note to inform Master Gunnery Sergeant Wilson.

Two men came in with their broken English, saying how nice of me to finally wake up. They said they would make it as painless as possible. I just needed to tell them where the vials were.

I looked at them, probably coming off defiant, but in reality, I was just trying to not black out again. My head was feeling lighter the longer I stayed up, and I said nothing. The stronger of the two cold-cocked me right across the jaw. I had no strength to withstand it and saw some of my teeth spraying out of my mouth. It took a special kind of individual to be able to hit a woman with such force. Not the kind you want to be left in a room with. They had no morals, conscious, or fiber of being human. They were robotic; they just performed. Just like Demi Moore in *G.I. Jane*, I responded with a "Suck my dick!"

The second of the two looked at me and said, "He'll continue until you tell him. He won't let you die until you do. But I'll be more merciful and will let it be quick." I guessed he was the good cop. I definitely thought I could take him, even in my current condition.

"I can't tell you what I don't know, so this is going to be quick." Another punch to my face, and this time, also my ribs. I knew he broke a few. Sweating profusely and trying to catch my breath, I felt more blood trickling down my face. I looked at Good Cop and laughed.

"What's so funny, Miss?"

"First of all, I think the phrase is: what's so funny, Missy? Second: at this rate, keep it up. I'm going to bleed out. You. Stupid. Ignorant. Shit." I knew I had to get the bleeding under control or I really was going to bleed out.

He came over and poured a sip of water into my mouth. My eyes were rolling to the back of my head and I spit a blood clot onto the floor. He apologized and said, "Sorry, I know you Americans like your wine more than water." What the fuck was he talking about?!

There were three men in what I called the observation room. Two more came in to join in the fun, leaving the Deputy Director in the room by himself. My eyes were swollen shut and I couldn't make out facial contexts, so strained to listen to their voices. One examined my head wound and yelled in Arabic to the bad cop to not hit my head, as they needed me alive. His voice sounded strangely familiar. He applied pressure to it, which stopped the bleeding momentarily.

Good Cop, trying to get his emotions in control, looked at me again and said, "I have all the time in the world. You, on the other hand, don't. Now, tell us where you put them."

"You really don't get it, do you? I don't have possession of them. I can't tell you where they are, and if I did have possession, how would you even know if I was telling you the truth?"

"We have our resources; we'd know."

"I'll tell you what you don't know: you don't know shit. You have the US Deputy Director yanking your chain, telling you all kinds of crap. Who do you think sent me here? Bingo. Now, why would he do that, when he could have done it in his own country versus coming to BFE."

It was doubtful they understood the acronym of 'bum fuck Egypt,' but I had their attention and they were looking at each other, debating. One seemed sympathetic to me. Just then, shithead came in and landed another punch square on me. I was out like a light.

I awoke to blaring music. Blood had crusted over my nose and mouth. My tongue was thick from the beatings. My eyes were swollen, almost unable to open. I could have been in Round 10 of any *Rocky* movie. My arms were aching from being pulled back and tied so tightly. I knew my time was limited and was still trying to come up with some scenario to get me out of this. There would be no Seal Team to come save me. I was on my own.

Once the men saw I was awake, all but one returned. Even my pal, ol' Deputy Director ('DD'), came in this time. His real name was Tom Bale, but I couldn't think of him as a Tom. He eyed me closely and circled around me to take it all in. Grandstanding. He wanted the others to think he was in control. "Matti, you will tell me what I need to know. Do you want to know why I'm so confident?"

"I'm not going anywhere, so why don't you fill me in."

He reached into his pocket and pulled out something small. My eyes were so swollen, I was having a hard time making out big objects, much less small ones. He slowly walked over to me, lifted my chin, and said, "My dear, I think I found something that belongs to you," and dangled the gold chain that my husband had given me. I screamed inside, trying not to let any emotion show, but felt utterly defeated. "It says 'Mama.' That's so sweet. How special; how very, very special. I just sent someone. We're locating your Tom and the kids now."

I didn't say a word. I just looked at him. Check-mate, he had me. He knew he had me, too.

People like me aren't just simply born this way; we are trained and conditioned. Maternal instincts are primal. We are born with them and it's natural to defend our own. I knew I had given Tom enough time to follow our plan in event of such occurrence, and Bethany and Tia would be there to help and protect them. I was confident they wouldn't find them. I couldn't control anything on the home front, but I could control what happened here.

This death wish rekindled a furor in me. I could withstand the pain; it was just physical and temporary. I needed more time. I wasn't sure what I was going to do, but I had to stay alive or hope to go quickly, so they couldn't get any information out of me. There was only so much pain a person could endure.

"It's taken you this long to get here, and what has it gotten you? Nothing. You are no further than where you started. You are pathetic and weak."

"Matti, I think you should consider who you are talking to. I am neither pathetic nor weak. I am a patient man, willing to wait years, even decades, to see things through completion. I will watch as all others die and we will rebuild a new nation from the throes of destruction."

Barely able to speak, I muttered, "Holy shit, Batman. I must be looking at the Joker. Let me see if I got this right. You're going to take the vials and put them in some kind of device to spread throughout nations, be it through water or air. A genocide. You go, boy; you ARE special. Want a sticker?"

One thing I knew about men: Attack their egos. I know to never let it become personal, but it did the moment he pulled out the necklace. I would have to fight a mental warfare right now, and hope to stall for a miracle.

He looked at me, trying to size me up, eyes narrowing, contemplating what to say. "While your astute summation is partly correct, you are missing the bigger picture. Tell me where the vials are, Matti. I will find them and then your family will be joining you shortly."

"If you don't mind, I'm going to catch me a few zzzs. You're giving me a headache." And I closed my eyes.

"Looks like we'll go the harder route. Fine with me. Let's start with the toenails and work our way up." With that, he motioned to the big bloke, who grabbed a pair of pliers and headed in my direction. This had to be divine intervention. Ever since sick fuck Miquel had clubbed my foot a few years back, I hadn't been able to feel anything in four out of my five toes on my left foot. Praise Jesus, please let him grab the left one. This was giving me time. I now needed a plan. I had two dart doses. If two men left, I could take two out. I would need to use the force of my legs to lift me up and jettison backwards, while pulling my hands up the side of bench to go over the bar, then bring them back so I could get my legs through, more than likely tearing my rotator cuffs in the process, get into my bra wiring with my hands still tied, pray that the dart tube had not warped because of the beatings and sweating, then split the reed, blow, and hope to take out two simultaneously. Grab their weapons and then proceed to take out the other two. F' me.

I knew I had to hold out. They made a mistake when they asked me twice and showed their weakness. They needed my information more than me being dead. Hulk wannabe came towards me. I stuck out my left foot purposefully to say 'bring it on.' He grabbed it and pulled it up to his knee level and opened the pliers. He looked at DD, who nodded to proceed. He yanked that pinky toenail straight off. I literally laughed out loud, as I could not feel a single thing. I kept laughing, now going into uncontrollable hysterics. He went in for the ring toe and did the same; all the while,

I was still laughing. DD was incredulous and you could see a vein popping out of his head. He went over, grabbed the pliers, and with full force, slammed it on my left femur. I felt that, alright...and passed out (again) from the pain.

I awoke to smelling salt, which rattled my already-throbbing head. DD and his three accomplices were looking at me. DD looked pissed. They were still all here, as my luck would have it.

"Matti, do you know what real power is? Have you ever witnessed it? What people will do to have it, to honor it, to protect it? These men here are willing to die for the greater good. These incompetent men who haven't been able to get you to divulge the vials' whereabouts understand what is necessary to prevail."

With that he motioned to Good Cop and Last Straggler to stand beside me. I was trying to brace myself for what the next round of torture would entail. What happened next literally blew my mind. Obediently, they both bent at the waist. DD came up to the first one and slit his throat from ear to ear. Blood spilled in all directions before he slumped over. The second one didn't flinch and DD did the same to him. I swear it was a scene out of *The Walking Dead*. It was so fucking surreal. He looked at me and said, "You will never understand true power."

I was in shock. And then I realized...down to just two men. Sign #2.

I now had a small bust of momentum and hope. "Bravo. You got rid of two worthless fucks. Big fucking deal."

'Enraged' would probably be the most accurate adjective for the moment. He wanted to break me and for me to be in awe. I was neither. I knew he wouldn't sustain this and ultimately would cave and probably just kill me now.

DD walked over and grabbed the blowtorch. My time was up. It was now or never for my plan, but there would be no way out unless I had a third miracle. I'd die in vain trying, though, and my last thoughts going through my head were hoping my family never had to find out what transpired here.

He slowly walked over to me with a grimacing smile. I looked in his hollow eyes. There was nothing. Deep breath in, deep breath out: in a few moments it will all be over. Eminem and Rihanna, *Love the Way You Lie,* played in my head...*Because I like the way it hurts...I love the way you lie...*

Just then, the lights went out. Holy shit. Miracle #3.

With no hesitation, I put all force on both legs to lift up, which was painful in itself, with my broken femur. I pulled my arms back to get under the seat back to pull them back around, under my legs, while throwing myself out from under the bench. Landing hard on my back, I had my tied hands at my bra, grabbing for the thin double tube inside it. I pulled the tubes apart to shoot individually and put one to my mouth to blow. I just needed a shot.

DD turned on the blowtorch, giving off enough light to see both him and Bad Cop. With missing teeth and swollen gums, I blew with all my might.

Chapter 17
Redemption

I heard a shot and thought that it was aimed at me. Then I felt a big whiff of air whoosh by as the ground shook with impact. The lights came back on. Bad Cop was on the floor with a round right in the middle of his head. My dart was nowhere near him. I lay on the floor, looking up to see a disheveled Fareed, who'd shot his last round from earlier.

I looked in the other direction. Lucky for me, my dart did hit the Deputy Director, who didn't know what had hit him. It feels like a small sting that numbs instantly and travels downward. Quickly, you are paralyzed from the serum and can't breathe from the paralysis. Oh, you're still awake for this. He was gasping for air, eyes bulging, spit spewing. I stared straight at him and mumbled, "What were you saying about power, now?" as he was unable to breathe.

I closed my eyes and said, "Well, hello, Possum." Fareed walked over to me, smiling. I loved this man. Not in a sexual way, mind you, but we bonded because of this experience. We looked at each other and both laughed just from the sheer gravity that had been lifted. It felt like the end of *Jaws*, where they laugh as they kick back to shore. He sat down beside me and we just sat there for a moment, taking it all in.

I finally broke the silence. "Glad you found me. I'm afraid I'm going to have to ask another favor, though."

"Goodness, woman, you really are pushing it," he said. "What now?"

"I can't move. You're going to have to get me out of here."

"This should be fun. I can barely move, myself."

"How did you find me?"

"I may be Possum, but it appears Freddy has nine lives..."

With the explosion, Fareed sustained his share of injuries, too, with part of the gear shift sticking to his collar bone and his internal organs smashed from impact. He knew his options were limited and hoped that by playing possum, they would just focus on me—and lucky for both of us, his acting skills prevailed, as they presumed him dead. He didn't know who to contact, as we both assumed Freddy was expired. His phone rang twelve hours later, and it was Freddy. Freddy didn't go into all the details with him on how he was able to maneuver out of his situation, but had a location on me, thanks to the tracking device in my head. They never scanned me for one when they brought me onto the tarp. I was not sure why; probably because my head was already split open. Rookie mistake.

Fareed had maneuvered in when he saw DD mow down the two by slitting their throats. His original plan was to come back with an arsenal, but he knew my time was limited and he had to act now. He was going to shoot the big one, grab his weapon, and then go for the other.

"That was your plan? You couldn't have brought another gun, at least, when you came?"

"In case you've missed it, I've had my share of cuts and bruises to attend to, also. I'm just thankful I don't look as bad as you."

"Let's get the fuck out of here. Give me your phone before I pass out. You need to dial. I can't see anything."

We called Freddy. I'd never been so happy to hear his voice, and I think the feeling was reciprocated when he heard mine. I told him the injuries sustained were substantial and we needed help getting out of not just the physical location, but the country, as well. He had already called my pals Jake and Steve, who were previously on mission over here, and diverted them to get us. They would be arriving any moment. Bless this man. Told him we'd have to catch up on the details later, as I was about to take a nose dive, with my head throbbing. I told him that Tom, my kids, and Bethany would be out of commission and on the run. He was relieved to hear I got word out to them before all this went down.

"Matti, you mentioned that one gentleman left the scene, correct? Were you able to see him?"

"Are you kidding me? My face is a punching bag. I couldn't see if it was my mother in front of me."

"I need to tell you something. Brace yourself. I think that was Aktar. Tom Bale wasn't the ringleader, but his first lieutenant, so to speak".

"He's going after my family, then, to locate the vials. I need to get out of here now. I need to go." And I hung up the phone.

Jake and Steve were there only moments later. Sure wish they could have been there from the start. My head was light. I knew I only had moments left before I would be unconscious again. As Jake bent down, I whispered in a broken garble, "Burn. It all. To the ground."

Steve, a trained paramedic as well, bandaged me up and had an IV going immediately. He put me in a self-induced coma for the transport. The boys took Fareed and me to Germany, to Landstuhl, where we would receive the best treatment. Unbeknownst to me, I would be in a coma for 14 days while the doctors worked on me.

Jake took pictures to show me, of Tom Bale burning. Just like I promised I'd see him. I needed to validate to anyone else that we'd all died in that explosion.

The doctors performed multiple surgeries. I spent six months at Landstuhl, recuperating and learning how to do basic motions again. Mentally, I was all there, but I had to learn to do the physical things again. The head impact was the largest of my issues, and temporarily impaired my speech and fine motor skills. It was frustrating and exhausting. Emotionally, I was all over the place with my family on the run. Freddy kept communication with them through US Postal Service. Just like in *Shawshank Redemption*, an occasional postcard would be sent. I can only imagine Tom's reaction when he received it. We could not take any chances and were on radio silence with them. I had to do this for their safety, despite it killing me inside.

Jake and Steve stayed until I was cleared from ICU. After that, I was in total isolation at Spa Landstuhl except for Fareed. Fareed was there every day until I left. A stranger became my closest trusted friend and confidant. I can never repay him for what he did to help me.

Each day, over in over in my head, I heard U2's *Song of Someone... I have some scars from where I've been... I was told that I would feel nothing the first time... I don't know how these cuts heal...*

I knew my return to my family would not be any time soon. For their protection, I had to eliminate all involved, at all costs. It was a pit in my stomach that fueled my desire and I constantly told myself that time was fleeting and this, too, would pass. I tried not to focus on the events that I was missing...holidays, birthdays, first dates, or even touchdowns. It was enough to drive anyone mad.

Before I could help anyone, I had to focus on my physical and mental rehabilitation. I had new body parts to get accustomed to and break in. As much as I wanted to dive in and start attacking, my new reality kicked in. This was going to be longer than I could have anticipated.
Freddy and I talked approach, targets, and outcome. We were still missing a key component on how they were going to distribute this, IF they got their hands on it. I had kept the vials for national security. My mom died for this. It was too powerful for any nation. Just as in the movie *Outbreak*, one little drop, and it was complete destruction. How were they going to distribute it was the key to locating the cell and eliminating all potential threats.

My head was muddled with conversations, trying to connect any dots. I woke up one morning with clarity. The subconscious worked its way.

I called Freddy.

He answered on the first ring. "I think I know how they are going to do it."

"What? How?"

"Remember that rope-a-dope years back, on the wine bottles mission?"

"Yeah, how does that tie into anything?"

"During my FUBAR experience, one of them made a statement. He said, 'Sorry, I know you Americans like your wine more than water.' I couldn't figure out what he was talking about or what the relevance was. We were looking for missile locations. What if we were looking at it all wrong? What if we should have been looking for distillery or distribution locations? Fifty percent of the world consumes alcohol, and most in wealthy nations. Some countries hardly drink at all, and where is that? In mostly Muslim locations. We were thinking in English when we were trying to decipher what ICBM and the codes meant. What if it was in Arabic?"

Long silence, as he was processing. Before he could speak, I said, "We need a full background on Tom Bale and how his connection tied into all of this and Aktar. Also, we need to know who has been purchasing and acquiring any of the big wineries in the last 10 years. Check Napa first, and start with the Gallos, Sterling, and bigger production wineries that distribute overseas, as well. Not high-priced wineries; high volume. See who is selling their grapes, as well, and to whom. I'll need transportation out of here; schedule it to leave tomorrow. It's time to start my rehab in the States."

"Are you sure you are up for this, Matti? Ten days ago, you were having problems buttoning your own shirt."

"Freddy, I can and I will."

Six months to the day, I left Landstuhl by myself. It was gut wrenching to leave Fareed, with whom I had spent so much time and who had become my closest ally. I had a private jet dump me in Atlanta. From there, I bought a car with cash. I didn't tell Freddy or anyone where I was heading, for all our best interests. I selected a small East Texas town so I could recuperate and strategize for the next events so I could return to my family and make them pay for the time I had missed. My head played *Kelly Clarkson's, Stronger...What doesn't kill you makes you stronger...what doesn't kill you makes a fighter...*

Chapter 18
T-minus

In my little haven in East Texas, I recuperated and rebuilt myself, not just physically, but mentally and emotionally. My "sit" room was a path of who's who, connecting dots and places. I reviewed footage and photos and anything else that I could get my hands on. Great thing about technology: you now could access remote locations. Bad thing about technology: they could access you, too. The ignorance the public had on social media. Ever since the Patriot Act, algorithms picked hundreds of thousands of key words and locations based on current events. I was redirecting satellites and bouncing off sites to get into encrypted areas. Information was king; applied knowledge was God.

My verbal conversations with Freddy were rare, now, due to security concerns, saving most context clues for different chat sites. You'd be surprise what you could decipher from online dating sites. My favorite place to post was farmersonly.com. If I was going to be holed up without my family, I had to keep my sense of humor. Bethany would receive coded messages from me from these sites and would knew to uproot my family again if she didn't hear from me. I forced myself not to spy on them through security or satellite surveillance, as I couldn't let this get emotional. It was already personal.

My library on Tom Bale grew extensive. I watched every speech and looked through thousands of photos, looking for hidden messages, trying to pinpoint the moment of conversion. At his high-ranking government level, he had to have a network supporting him. This was no one-man operation, but an intricate, intertwined coup. Was Tom our own Liv Schreiber in *The Manchurian Candidate*? A programmed vessel?

Locating the elusive Aktar was more challenging. Despite every attempt, no photos of him surfaced; just rumored stories of his whereabouts and conversations. A new theory emerged. There was no Aktar. Despite tremendous governmental resources being allocated to the elaborate hunt and location of him and his cell group, it was to a diversion. Another rope-a-dope. False sense of security, allowing the public to think he was the reason why terrorism existed.

Six months after my release, I had made progress on the distribution theory, tracking down the players at large and potential outcomes. Where I was still falling short was connecting some of those dots. I was missing a key. I traveled to Louisiana and called Freddy.

With relatively no interaction with anyone for six months, I was always relieved when I did get to speak with Freddy, which was very infrequent. We had to keep our conversation length to a minimum, as we bounced off multiple relays. I would fill him in my findings and theories and vice versa. Nothing new was to be reported and I was feeling despondent, knowing time was ticking away from my family.

As we hung up, Freddy mentioned that he'd paid off the last of the nurses/doctors/hospitals, and based off what was paid, I was more costly than the Six Million Dollar Man and Bionic Woman combined. I laughed and told him I was worth it and reminded him that some of those costs were probably Fareed's, too. I wasn't expecting his response.

"Fareed wasn't treated."

"Freddy, are you absolutely sure? What about his collarbone? Was he treated somewhere else?" I asked.

"Per Jake and Steve's report, he sustained no injuries and he never left your side while you were in ICU or afterwards."

Breathe in. Breathe out.

"Freddy, we never discussed this in detail, but where did they capture you, and how did you get out of the situation?"

"I was outside the Pentagon. I had two face-masked men on me in the parking lot. Things we are trained for, as they threw me in an unmarked van. It was a complete surprise. I was blindfolded and bound. We drove for roughly 20 minutes when we came to an abandoned barn. They didn't do anything. No interrogation, no injury. We sat there in silence for hours. Suddenly, they left in a hurry and I had two Department of Defense guys there, releasing me, saying they were alerted when I didn't make a scheduled appointment, and they tracked me to the location."

"Just like that and it was over? Were you able to track down any additional information after?"

"I tried based-off surveillance, where I ended up, and speech dialect, but ended with nothing," he said.

"The two men who rescued you, they work for Bale?"

"Yes, and were killed in action on a mission shortly after my release."

"How did you connect me to Fareed?"

"His twin brother, Abdul, has worked for the US since practically birth."

I've always been fascinated with name origins. You are given a name by your parents, but there does seem to be a certain destiny that is applicable to some. Abdul means Servant of God. I had no idea Fareed had a twin.

"Freddy, you'll need to make a call. I need to make a few, too."

Chapter 19
Armageddon

When Miquel Badham landed on my doorstep, it left only a handful of possibilities. Since he was unable to communicate any confirmation of a kill or capture, because of his ultimate demise, the next chain of events would unfold.

It had been roughly 24 hours since he landed at my driveway and technically started becoming one with the pond, lake, fire pit, and yard. Bless his heart. Within 8 more hours, I could expect to find additional unwanted guests arriving. How many, I didn't know, but I could guarantee their arrival. They would need time to prepare for this operation and would want to wait till nightfall for the element of surprise. There was no surprise, since they sent Miquel in first, as a scout.

I could always flee, but that wouldn't resolve the issue and wouldn't get me back to my family. Plus, I liked this house. Maybe I could convince Tom and the kids to move here after this was all done.

I took a quick power nap as the dogs watched over me. I knew I'd need all my strength for later. Not only did I prep the house inside and out for what was about to come; I tried to prepare myself mentally. I fell asleep listening to the theme song from *Apocalypse Now* by the Doors, *The End*.

I awoke and did some quick prep reading:

Ecclesiastes 7:9
Do not be quickly provoked in your spirit, for anger resides in the lap of fools.

My daily Bible verse was quite inspirational and a reminder of things to come, don't you think? I took it as a sign. I said a quick prayer. "Lord, have mercy on them, for I won't. Amen."

The problem with setting a trap was it was like killing off rats. Once you put out bait, they all come. You must eliminate them all if you want to get rid of them. If you didn't, you wasted your time, as they will multiply and continue to return. Reminded me of that children's book: *If you give a mouse a cookie...*they're going to want a glass of milk.

I took my time getting dressed, carefully selecting the appropriate attire. I needed maneuverability, but concealing. I wore my hair pulled down over my ears in a low pony. No contacts or disguises this go around, au natural, so to speak.

I double checked my security measures. Although I wanted to carry my Colt Python, I opted for more silent options, with DTA Stealth recons set up on both sides of the front entry. My weapon of choice for personal carriage was a Hudson H9, which gave me 15-round double-stack mag rounds and low bore axis with less recoil and muzzle rise when shooting. It was designed for precision.

Now it was a matter of time. I made myself a quick sandwich and headed to my office, or what I called the 'sit room.' I was about to test some of this new state-of-the-art technology by blowing some unwanteds to kingdom come.

Five acres of heavily treed lot is harder than you think, to scan and be vigilant over. I had the dogs with me and would almost swear that they were scanning the video footage, too, as they were on heightened alert. I was scanning through the neighbor's surveillance, as well. Minutes turned into hours. Time, the ultimate killer. Made you doubt, heightened anxiety, and controlled your emotions, if you let it. Not today: *I'm an oak*, as Doc Holliday would have said.

Tick tock. Now it neared 1:00AM. I had several screens up and programmed to flag for any motion. Something just caught my eye. It was there and then gone. I watched and waited some more. One minute turned into fifteen. Bingo. There it was again. Seemed they were communicating by pen-sized flashlights, of all things. And after a few seconds...there it was...the return across the other side of lake. I now had two locations and remote controlled the Recons to position accordingly. No light was on in my house, not even an appliance light, and where I was located inside, no light could be seen. It was pitch black.

Light and darkness could play key factors in missions. One's ability to acclimate or assimilate was greatly impacted by the absence or presence of light. I was counting on it tonight to aid in my efforts.

Tick tock. They were moving in slowly, but I had their locations on target. I had to wait; there were other factors in play, now. I counted at least 12. I suspected more likely 30. Three words. *Bring it on.* Well, really 4 or 5 words: *Bring it on, motherfuckers.* Was that hyphenated, or two words? You get my point.

Breathe in, breathe out. A quick Serenity prayer – *God grant me the serenity to accept the things I cannot change, the courage to change the things I can; the wisdom to know the difference. Oh, and to be dead on balls accurate in every shot.*

I looked down to Koda and Bruiser. *"It's time, boys, Place."* With that, they carefully maneuvered to the outskirts of the room. 3.2.1 – lights on. Not in my house, nor around it, which was still pitch black; but the lights I had installed on outside perimeter property line in the far parts of the lot that now beaconed in on them, putting them in the wide open. With night vision goggles, they had a shutoff to protect the tube. These wouldn't damage your eyes, despite what the movies portrayed, but it was a nuisance and hassle to mess with, as it took time to acclimate to a new environment. Just like when you turn off all the lights at home, it takes your eyes a second before you can acclimate and start to see. It also helps when you have a working knowledge of the area. You know where your couch is, so your memory recall assists. It's only natural for any individual to momentarily freeze before you must compute to scatter, attack, or change intentions. I wouldn't be able to get all of them, based on their individual decisions, but I didn't need that. Twenty or so, and they all dispersed. First a muffled sound, and then a thud. Followed by another, and another, and another. I'm sure they weren't suspecting this. I had to smile. I personally hadn't laid a finger on any trigger. Yet.

Lights off. Pandemonium. I'm telling you, light and dark can really mess with your abilities. Especially when you have no control. Another thud, and then another. Lights on. I thought about Mr. Miyagi, "wax on, wax off." Six down. Lights off. Damn, maybe I'm like Claire Danes in *Homeland* and am just a bipolar manic depressant? Time to focus; it was about to be my turn and there was no room for mistakes.

Pursuers were now coming at full force, weaving in and out of the trees while shooting at anything in front and behind them for their protection. The property line was breached, so it was only a matter of time before someone busted through my door. My only advantage was that they needed me alive so I knew they wouldn't drop an aerial missile and blow it all up.

I needed them closer for the next tactics. As some approached through the back, I blew the Boston Whaler, which took out 7, 8, and 9. I finally pulled the trigger on the Recons and took out 10, 11, 12, and 13. It felt like in the movie *Inception*, all going in slow motion, but me understanding every next move.

Arsenal was coming in now, and my pristine house was taking a massive hit with glass shattering everywhere. Damn it, I was pissed. Take that, 14 and 15, who were sliced. Number 16 landed on the coyote trap, and had a leg dangling before he had his screams squelched with a round to the head. Numbers 17 and 18 started backtracking before they saw their demise.

Then, nothing. All was silent. Time for my big girl pants, and to bring this home. They were close. I mean, I was good, don't get me wrong, but I couldn't follow 30 all at one time. Sheez.

And then I heard it through a bull horn: "Matti, stop before you shoot someone you love."

My heart sank just from his voice. Why did I always have to be right?

From his voice, I aimed the Recons over to his direction. Lights on. And there he stood, all 5'8 of him, flanked by 19 through 29 and holding 30 in front of him.

"I wouldn't do that, Matti. I'd hate to have to get your family involved, next. You're a smart woman; you know how this plays out."

Yes I did, fucker; yes I did.

I pressed the outside intercom and said, "Come on in, Possum." Who knew how accurate this identifier would be, as he had been adept at surviving in diverse locations and conditions, just like the actual marsupial. To me, possums were just big rats.

Fareed didn't move. His .44 Magnum revolver was sure to have the trigger guard removed for faster firing and was pointed upward at the base of her neck. The gun with its extended barrel length looked ridiculous in his small hands; obviously, he had his own size issues. I had planned on him carrying his other S&W, but I think he was trying to go Dirty Harry on me. Unless he was suicidal, he wasn't going to pull it just yet. He knew the value of his hostage. He had spent decades on this quest. He was crazy, not stupid.

He wouldn't be coming in just yet; he knew I would have the advantage, once he was inside the house. It was time to see how well I could act. I waited 30 seconds and came to the door, no weapon in sight, and lifted my hands.

"Fareed, why are you doing this? This won't have a good conclusion for any involved. Bethany, you look great as always, love. I sure have missed you, whop-eye." And with that I gave my best and dearest friend a sincere and genuine smile. She returned a tired but trusting look, with who knew what had been going on for the last 24 hours. I could never repay her for all that she has done for me and my family. I would kill for her.

"I think I've been patient enough, Matti. Give me what I came for, and I'll only kill you and her, versus your whole family."

How ridiculous. He knew it wouldn't be that easy. Oh, ok, I'll give it to you now. Good grief. I waited and finally said, in a calm and disgusted tone, "I trusted you. I considered you a friend; all the while you were like Raul Julia in *Tequila Sunrise*, being the double agent and having everyone look for someone else while you were leading the charge. Bravo, good work...well, up until the last 24 hours, that is."

"You work with the CIA and FBI and other government agencies; you should know better than to trust anyone.

After years of being profiled, I became exactly what you all concluded I would be. This is on all of you."

Dr. Finkelstein, we can forget about Mom for a while, we have a whole new bag of issues.

"Spare me, Fareed. You'll need to accept your own accountability on this one. YOU had a choice, you've chosen who you are – and I'm disappointed to learn, you ARE nothing."

He pulled the .44 from her head and aimed it towards me. It was a 100-yard shot. I had scripted this. We discussed what Bethany and I could do to take out the others and him, but the potential loss outweighed the gain. We had no idea how many he would have with him at this point, and needed to ensure the safety of my family with Abdul still at large. He pulled the trigger, which hit my right shoulder area squarely. I jolted from the direct hit and red ooze appeared and trickled down my arm.

I hunkered down from the impact at first and then grabbed my shoulder and straightened back up. "Good shot, looks like it went right through. Glad to see that you aimed for my firing arm. Smart thinking. I'm just glad it wasn't my left side. Maybe now, I can even out in my injuries."

"The next shot won't be so lucky for you, or for her. If you want, I can make a call now and you can listen as your husband and kids go first. Is that what you want?"

The thing with bluffing is: you need to be able to carry it through, regardless. The main way to know if one is bluffing is to know what hand the other player has. Or doesn't.

"Let's go inside, then. Bring your body idiots with you." I looked over to the soulless-looking fools and said, "By the way, nice job, boys. You have been chosen, and you and the aliens will go on to a better place." Fareed motioned for four of them to follow him inside while the rest stood guard outside.

Two blockheads came beside me with triggers aimed at both front temples. I thought of myself as Doublemint gum just then, with a double-your-pleasure movement going on. As we maneuvered through the front door, I stated matter-of-factly, "I must admit, I'm a little pissed. You shot my beautiful home to pieces. Don't cut yourself on the glass. I'd hate for you to accidentally bleed out. Watch your step."

"Get to it, Matti. Where is it?"

I gingerly walked through the main foyer, slowly making my way into the kitchen, avoiding the glass and wreckage. "Can I at least patch this up for a moment?" I grabbed for a paper towel to put up to my shoulder. "I don't get it, Fareed. You stayed with me for 6 months. Why? Patience is one thing, but that bordered on absurd. And then I realized why. You didn't want me to find out it was you. You were either ashamed or smitten. Maybe both. Maybe neither; it doesn't matter, as a crack developed. Looks like one of the deadliest sins got involved, Pride. From that, it appears you manifested more of Anger, Envy, Lust and Greed. Shit, you're just missing Sloth and Gluttony at this point."

"You always did talk like a sailor. It's unbecoming. Stop stalling, Matti." His voice was calm, and he pulled Bethany with him as we moved further into the house. "In those 6 months, I realized what mattered to you—your family and your country. We both sacrifice for a higher purpose. I admire your tenaciousness and blinding loyalty to a country that is self-obsessed and self-destructive. Who are you to lecture me on the deadly sins? Maybe you have been holed up here a little too long. Maybe you should follow your own Presidential election process."

"Don't compare us as the same. You are a terrorist. You're using violence for control. So that justifies what you want to do? What do you call it? Global cleansing? Are you the new God in this new world, or who is—maybe it's your twin brother, Abdul?" I WAS stalling. I needed a little more time and to position for the right angle.

His eyes were piercing, his teeth grinding, as he narrowed down on me. I swear I felt like he was thinking about that Nine Inch Nails *Closer* song as he stared at me...*I want to feel you from the inside...* "It took you long enough to connect the dots. It won't matter to you; you won't be part of it."

"Wow, that hurts. I thought we were friends." He was right, though. It did take way too long to figure this out. I felt like Olivia Pope in *Scandal*, where it always took her to the end of the show to figure out what was right in front of her. Damn, that bites. It was time for part two of this to start, and I casually glanced over at Bethany.

Just like in the *Italian Job*, we had orchestrated every little detail. We'd discussed every outcome and planned for the expected and unexpected.

"Let her sit down, Fareed, and follow me. Let's get this over with."

Fareed looked over at Bethany, who was barely moving, exhausted and in pain. He motioned to two of the guys to set her down and then added to shoot her if she moved. He then told the other two to follow us. Everything was going to plan.

My sit room was a high-tech panic room designed by Burton Safes, offering the highest level in security, and was meticulously engineered. To top it off, it was luxurious in a James Bond way. The entrance door was designed to retain the style of the property and to blend in effortlessly, while offering a fire and ballistic level to meet my specific needs. This was no 12x12 room but an 800-square-foot suite ensemble with the pinnacle leading to a Dottling Grand Circle masterpiece on the back wall. It is one of the most expensive safes in the world, with certified fire protection and 52 individually controlled watch winders, jewelry drawers, an air humidifier, and the topper: an exclusive kick-ass mini bar. James Bond would have given his approval on this. It reminded me of Vegas with a 2-meter-high large black and Spanish cedar Pendulum clock on top of a sophisticated high-gloss lacquered base table. I tried to purchase the Dottling Narcissus, designed by Karl Lagerfield himself, but there were only 30 produced and I couldn't afford to draw attention to the purchase. The Grand Circle was a work of art.

We walked inside and Fareed looked around incredulously. "You appear to have exquisite taste, I'll give you that. You couldn't just have a Worthington 1000 safe, could you?"

I grabbed my shoulder and winced in pain. "There's still time, Fareed; you don't have to do this."

"I have spent decades in the search for this and finally, now at the conclusion, you really think I'm going to change my mind?" he stammered.

"Yes. Yes, I do."

"You're a fool, then. You were right, though. I instantly liked you when we met. You do possess a certain charm. It's your confidence that is so appealing and I knew it would lead to your downfall. I knew if I could become close, eventually you would finally lead me to what is rightfully mine. For generations, my country has been searching for what your mother stole from us. It's personal. An eye for an eye."

The mention of my dead mother made my blood boil. Oh, it was personal, motherfucker, I knew that. To think of his people that he sacrificed. I was not talking to my friend Fareed, who'd sat by me for months, but to a deranged psychopath. As I've always said, you can't reason with crazy. It was time. This had gone on long enough.

"Do what you must do," I said, and motioned to the Grand Circle.

It was like holding peanut butter in front of a dog, to see his eyes glisten and basically salivate. It could have been scripted from any Indiana Jones movie. He walked over in awe, arms stretched, still holding on to his revolver. He touched it ever so gently, caressing it. He had arrived at the climax of his delusion and was basking in its glory. When he couldn't take it anymore, he turned to me and said, "Open it."

"It's your rodeo. You open it."

"If you pull any tricks, if there is any backlash, they will hurt you beyond what you just endured, and you will watch as they painfully kill your friend and your family. You will come to know pure evil. Do we understand each other?"

"Open it, Fareed; this is what you have been waiting for. We both know what happens next."

For him to open the Grand Circle, it would require him to put down his gun and use both hands. He stopped and motioned to the two others to come closer as they stood guard beside me, having me directly behind him, now. He laid down his gun on the right-hand side of the base table and proceeded to open his destiny.

Behind him, I could feel the adrenaline rushing; the longing; the awakening on his part and on mine. As he reached out to open it, I whispered...

"Fareed, one last thing before you open it... Attack."

I feel it's a *Blow Up the Outside World* by Soundgarden kind of day...*Nothing seems to kill me no matter how hard I try...And nothing seems to break me...Nothing can break me at all...*

Chapter 20
Debrief

It all came down to the little details. It turned out that Fareed was an actor himself from the get go, but the small momentous oversight on medical attention to his injuries, or lack thereof, ended up bringing this to a conclusion. Therefore, either he wasn't really injured, or his twin brother Abdul was in the accident with me and Fareed joined us later at FUBAR. Who knows. What I did know was that the fifth person in the room who wasn't identified was either him or Abdul. They were the elusive and imaginary Aktah.

I had Freddy reach out to Fareed and tip him off that he was worried about my mental welfare and stability, having been isolated for so long, and I was in desperation mode to return to my family. Maybe having Fareed as a friend to come visit me would help provide some comfort and relief. They had been in contact since my "relocation," as Fareed would reach out to check on my status, so it would not be out of the ordinary for Freddy to contact him. We needed bait, so Freddy dangled that Bethany was the only one who knew my actual location.

Before Freddy contacted Fareed, I had already called Bethany and informed her what we needed to do with Tom and the kids, while not alerting them to any danger. She, in turn, would have Tia take them to the next vacation destination in Coronado, California, which happened to host the Navy Seals training center, and they would be surrounded by the best of the best on their "field trip" and potentially extended stay-cation.

I reached out to Jake and Steve and told them I needed to enlist their services. We conferenced with Bethany and Freddy and worked out all the details. Freddy had grave concerns regarding the number of people Fareed would recruit with him, but I had full confidence in Jake and Steve's abilities to handle anything outside the perimeter of the house and was reluctant to bring in any additional unknown personnel, especially in light of the fact that this had inside governmental involvement.

Bethany, on the other hand, would be the one we would have to maneuver and improvise with the most, with the unknown being how Fareed would treat her. I was confident he would not kill her, but the inherent risk was substantial. She didn't hesitate on the plan.

I felt Fareed would want to do some physical harm on me. Not because he wanted to hurt me, but to validate to himself that he could prevail and didn't have any emotional ties that would hinder him from finishing his quest. I was counting on a Florence Nightingale effect, hoping he'd started having feelings for me during my stay at Landstuhl.

Freddy's target was Abdul. After he was located, he was to track and keep his eyes on Abdul and join him after we knew where Bethany had been taken. Fareed would want to tie up loose ends and tell Abdul to dispose of Freddy as well.

From this, our strategy was simple. It all came down to directing others to where we wanted them to be, when we wanted them to be there.

Bethany left herself in a position to be taken hostage. From there, after some time, she gave up my location. Fareed sent psycho Miquel Bandham to investigate first. You remembered how he ended up, right? Fish food. With location verified, but no communication, Fareed was enraged and Bethany played to his ego to come with an arsenal by confronting his inability to resolve it after all these years. She sustained a few whacks on that, but luckily, not as much as she had acted. I swear, we needed to win some Oscars after all this shit. Abdul surfaced to meet Fareed, and that's when Freddy intervened.

Jake and Steve were positioned in my neighbor's deer blinds and were able to take out the first 6 intruders. They had eyes on Fareed and directed him and some of his posse to proceed within the perimeter of the house as they continued to shoot, forcing them to breech. Fareed had 10 come in with him, so Jake and Steve would be responsible for any that remained outside of the house. I knew Fareed would leave the lion's share outside, based on his paranoia. Jake and Steve were well armed and had higher ground.

Now, for my part. I prepped the house for what needed to blow, the outside lights, and secured the most lightweight cutting-edge body armor, made for me by Kuyoshi. I knew that if Fareed tried to shoot me, outside of my head, that it wouldn't penetrate; but don't kid yourself, it would be quite painful. I also knew that my special effects would have to be on point, and stole some material from the movie *F/X*. I always complained to Fareed that all my injuries happened on my left side. When he shot me on my right side, it confirmed to me at least that he had some compassion towards me. I was not sure if that was subconscious or not, on his part, but I was prepared either way. Koda and Bruiser would play an invaluable part at his conclusion.

When Bethany sat on the couch, she laid down, feigning exhaustion, and grabbed the S&W460XVR under the armchair pillow. I thought it would only be fitting to have her use the same model gun that Fareed was accustomed to shooting.

When Fareed and his two guns followed me to my sit room, all parties could hear my conversation and were given context clues as to timing, as we were all wearing earpieces, which my wonderfully coiffed hair covered. Just as in *Silence of the Lambs*, Clarice was trained that you needed to clear the back of the room. Fareed and his two idiots didn't even notice the dogs in the corners of the room. They didn't move; you couldn't even hear them breathe.

When I said the word NEXT, it gave each a party the parameter of a three-second countdown, with ATTACK being the ultimatum finish. We were aiming to have it all conclude at the same time, so no communication could come out from their end.

Jake and Steve lit up the grounds and put mowing down to an all-time new level. Think *Goodfellas* with silencers. Jake flanked them from the left, while Steve moved from the right. Men weren't getting out of there alive, much less the new sod I had laid down. Damn it.

Bethany had two bullets in the foreheads of her captors before they could even think "oh fuck."

That left me. The dogs were on command and fastidiousness as they leapt and clutched the jugulars of the two in their mouths, leaving them spewing blood across the room. At the same time, I grabbed the .44 with my right "injured" hand. The white in Fareed's eyes were wide and fearful as he instantaneously realized his pursuit of a lifetime had just been terminated with foreshadowing of his ultimate demise.

"You always impress me with your resiliency. I have to give you that," he said as his arm dropped to the base table and he leaned forward in defeat.

"Open it up; see what you will be missing."

His opaque eyes lingered ever so heavily on his pending failure. To have it so close and not be able to come to fruition. He opened it with frailty, beaten, but wanting to see what it could have been. There was nothing but a post-it note. His eyes were baffled, trying to calculate the meaning, and he hesitantly grabbed and read, "I'm sorry, I can't, don't hate me." Bam, straight from *Sex and the City*. Confused by the meaning, he turned to me and stated, defeated, "It was never here, was it?"

"Have you ever heard the phrase, if you give a mouse a cookie, it's gonna want a glass of milk? It's from a children's book, but I realized...I first heard it from Harrison Ford in *Air Force One*. (It still gives me chills when he says "Get off my plane" and then they say "Liberty 24 is changing call signs, Liberty 24 is now Air Force One.") The irony is: you'll never know how close and how far you really were to finding it. Sometimes we covet what is right in front of us and it blinds us from reality."

I lost him on that one.

"Get it over with, Matti," he said as he pointed to the revolver I was holding.

I aimed the muzzle at his head as he closed his eyes and then shot him in the shoulder, the same place he'd thought he shot me. Wringing with pain, he grabbed his shoulder and grimaced, all the while looking at me, pleading. "Get it over with!"

"Oh, you must have me confused with someone who has mercy. That's God's department, not mine. We could argue that it would be easier and faster just to end it, but then, what kind of example does that leave for others? Oh no...I won't be killing you today. In fact, I will watch and witness as you are imprisoned in our legal process for the remainder of your life. You'll be in isolation for the duration, not even able to use a real fork or have shoelaces. Probably hard to give yourself a good hand-jerk with that injury you just sustained. Of course, if you did make it out to general population, you could look forward to rape and sodomy from the same people you wanted to cleanse the world of. At your size, you'll make a nice little bitch."

"It will never come to that; you know that as well as I do. Those who don't fear death, never die."

"Ahh, sadly, you are right. That's also why I'm not killing you today, as much as it pains me. You deserve to die, but not today. We—that would be the US. We need to dangle you as a cookie, to catch others. Once we've used you, I'll happily pull the trigger myself." With that, I slammed the revolver butt into the back of his head, knocking him out.

Just then, Jake, Steve and Bethany came in. My eyes lit up and I had a smile on my face. My extended family was here in the flesh. It had been so long. We safely secured Fareed, bandaged up his shoulder, and then Steve doped him up enough to go comatose. I asked the boys, "We get word from Freddy?"

"Yep, all in motion," said Jake.

"Wait, hold up. What's in motion?" inquired Bethany.

"Sorry, B, I didn't fill you in on this part. We had Freddy let Abdul go."

"You did what?!" she exclaimed, sounding just like the late great Bill Paxton in *Aliens*.

"It doesn't end with just them. I wish it did. They've infiltrated our government and our agencies. They've corrupted our society with fear and misteachings. I'm afraid we're just getting started."

"Are you high? Do you know what I just went through while you were "recuperating"? How about driver's ed with not one, not two, but three teenage kids. All at the same time! No, no, no, thank you. You stay home with your grieving husband next time and I'll go out. And your parents; let's not forget about them and their daily calls asking for updates. And, you failed to mention you had a creepy Uncle Eric from your dad's side. AND..."

She went on ranting for a full 10 more minutes. The boys and I didn't say a word, but looked back and forth to each other, occasionally with a smile.

When she finally had a stop in her momentum, I looked her in the eyes and grabbed her hands. "Bethany, I'm truly sorry. I can never repay you for everything you have done for me and my family. You are my family. I love you." And I waited for just a second before I added, with a huge smirk, "Ready to hug it out?"

"Don't think it's going to be that easy. We're just getting started. I have a list of shit you'll need to do to make amends with me."

"I'm sure you do. Come on, Whop-eye. Let's get the hell out of here."

With that, we all started out. The boys had their vehicle up the road and Steve had brought it back down to the property, where they loaded Fareed in the back. He wouldn't be moving for a while. They offered to take the dogs with them until I could come get them. I looked at my friends and hugged them and thanked them again. "Love you, boys, chat soon. Real soon. We have some work ahead of us. Be good to my dogs." They kindly reminded me again that they'd stopped counting how many times they had to cover or protect my ass. As they turned to jump in their vehicle, I started singing, *"We're the Four Best Friends that anyone could have, and we'll Never ever ever ever leave Each other."* Steve immediately chimed in and joined in with the next verse while Jake and Bethany protested vehemently over our tone-deaf singing before Jake sped out to take Fareed to his new resting place.

I had no idea what story I was going to tell my neighbor Gary on the mess at the house and property and was just glad that he was out of town so I could have a crew sent in. Luckily, no one blew up my Jag in all the destruction, and I jumped into the driver's seat. I finally got to drive this car out in the daylight. Bethany looked at me while rolling her eyes (if you could call it that). "You really need help. I could quote movie lines and lyrics all day, too, if I hadn't been raising someone else's kids 24x7 for the last 365 days...."

It was going to be a long ride home. I couldn't wait.

All I want to do is a Vroom, vroom...

Chapter 21
Homecoming

Tom and the kids were situated in Whitefish, Montana, a small town of less than seven thousand. Only twenty-six percent of the households had children under eighteen, which I knew would be problematic for the kids, but there was also less than five percent with a female household with no present husband. Just saying. Whitefish was a resort town, with many transient people, including my family. Part of the Rocky Mountains, it was a gateway to lakes and mountains. It was a hop, skip and jump to Canada, too, so that was a bonus in the consideration, if another fast getaway was needed. No one would be looking for them here.

The high school served a total of 500 students with class sizes at a 15:1 ratio. The triplets, with all their training, would be like Clark Kent or Dash from *The Incredibles,* trying to conceal their true performances and identities. I'm sure Tia would have them using the great outdoors to their advantage.

Tom had opened another franchise here which catered to the uber-wealthy people who had large second and/or third homes here, to get away from the real world. This kept him preoccupied, which we both needed. Although I had not permitted myself to put actual surveillance on him or the kids, I was able to monitor his activity every day through my favorite workout routine, good ol' faithful Peleton. I could see which classes he took, and how hard he'd trained. One time, the instructor called him out for his 500th class and I wanted to jump through like the *Matrix* just to touch him. I saw the days he did multiple rides, and each holiday he did the scenic rides (always to Napa), and I hoped he was reminiscing about me.

It was a 30-hour car ride from Texas. It seemed like an eternity, but then again, not enough time to figure out what to say. How do we ever recover completely? Would it all be different? Could it ever be the same? How could I kill people with no emotion, but have my nerves wrecked, thinking of this? How much have the kids grown? Would they be spiteful? Could I take it if they were? I would have to learn to accept my fate. I did this.

Bethany filled me in on everything on the long ride, from how the kids were coping to how they were doing at school. Who they liked and who they didn't. Over and over, she mentioned how impressed she was with the kids and especially Tom's perseverance and resiliency. I had a pit in my stomach.

As we approached closer, dread became fear, and fear became anxiousness. *Breathe in, breathe out.* We drove up the long winding road and I could see the house situated on the top of the hillside in majestic splendor. They didn't scrimp on finances here. The autumn leaves were turning colors with breathtaking views of the foliage and pristine lake. The house was three floors from the backside with massive windows facing the impressive view. You could see a fireplace on the top floor balcony and fire pits on each of the other floors. Tom always was a sucker for fire. I must admit, it did give it an exquisite appeal.

It was dark outside when we turned the last of the road into the front driveway. Bethany turned to me and said,

"Go in. I'm going to run to the store and will be back by tomorrow. By the way, I failed to mention to you that you purchased me a nice home just down the street." Touché.

"What do you think I should say first?" I asked in almost a begging tone.

"How about starting with hello," she stated matter-of-factly. "Now, get out; I've had enough of you for now."

I got out and handed her the keys. I eyed the house and closed my eyes for a moment, silently willing myself to face what was ahead with courage and wisdom. I walked to the door and saw Bethany pulling out. I sat at the door and counted 3.2.1, then rang the doorbell.

The front door was a mammoth wood double door, surrounded by glass on each side so you could see a person walking through the entryway. No one was approaching, but I could hear muffled sounds inside. I waited a few more seconds and then rang the bell again.

Tom appeared and walked towards the door. He had grown a groomed beard that covered his face. It looked really good on him. He looked really good. He was leaner than before, but still muscular. His walk was confident, but natural. What was I going to say?

He opened the door and we stared at each other, our eyes telling a lifetime story between us. For the first time ever, I wasn't convinced I knew what he was thinking. It felt like minutes, but only a second or two had passed. I finally blurted out, "Hello," the only thing I could muster.

He stood staring at me with a twinkle now in his eye. I broke down, grabbed him, and poured out, in sobbing hysterics, "I'm so sorry it's taken me this long. I would have never gone had I had known; please forgive me. I'm so sorry."

I was still crying when he gently pulled my head up and lingered as he looked at me, caressing my face, wiping the tears away from my eyes, and finally bending down to give me a kiss on my forehead, on my cheeks, and finally on my lips. It was…heaven. My eyes were red and swollen, but relief flooded over me. He massaged my hair back and said, "You had me at hello." God, I loved this man. "You look good as an auburn. Come inside; the kids have been anxious to see you."

My heart was pounding as I entered. Damn, he really had better decorating taste than me. I was going to have to keep working to sustain this lifestyle.

The triplets came running in, with the boys picking me up from both sides and Mary holding onto my legs. We laughed and cried and I never wanted to let go. After a while, they showed me around and talked in earnest as they filled me in on the house and school. We went around to each of the colossal rooms as they introduced me to the house. They showed me the guest suite that Tia used when she came over each day to continue their studies. Each of them looked like they had grown 6 inches, with both the boys over six feet and Mary at 5'9. Mark was still taller than Matthew, and was still enjoying it immensely. Suddenly, they all exclaimed in delight that they needed to show me the best part of the house. With an inquisitive look, I looked back at Tom, who was sheepishly smirking. I wasn't sure what to make of it, but they opened the door to the game room where two large labs came bouncing to the door, nearly knocking us all over. One was pure white, while the other was a striking red. The dogs jumped up and down and circled around, while the kids squealed with joy and excitement. I looked at Tom and laughed, "You got us two dogs while I was gone?"

"They aren't good guard dogs; they're more likely to run away with you if you offer them a treat, and will be the first to kick you off the sofa, but they're family now."

"Well, our family will be growing, as I got two more coming our way." The kids jumped up and down, asking for all the details. Mary showed me on her phone no less than 300 pictures of the dogs.

Tom ordered food and we all talked, and talked, and talked. By 1:00 AM, I was yawning and Tom told the kids they needed to go to bed and let Mom rest up. I was exhausted, but in a good way. The kids hugged me again while pleading with me not to leave ever again. It broke my heart.

Tom grabbed my hand and led me to the bedroom and showed me where he put all my things. Damn, he really did have great taste. I jumped into the shower while he went to grab us water. When he returned, he was leaning on the bed with a peaceful look.

"Come hither, Mrs. Baker."

When I Said I Do by Clint Black plays in my head...*It always looks the same, true love always does...When I said I do...I meant that I will 'til the end of all time...*

Epilogue

Fall turned into winter and we were covered by many feet of white protruding snow. Between hiking, snow-boarding and fire pit romps, we stayed busy with all the outdoor activities. The kids were busy with their various activities and I realized how much I'd missed the daily conversations when I had to drive them.

Fareed was quickly sentenced to life with no fanfare and placed at a "supermax" federal prison in Colorado—the United States Penitentiary, Administrative Maximum Facility (ADX); or the Alcatraz of the Rockies, as it was referenced. It contained some of the most dangerous male inmates in the world. It houses roughly 400 inmates and has included foreign terrorists, including Zacarias Moussaoui, the only person convicted in the 9/11 attacks. Many waited out their term here before being transferred to Terre Haute, which housed the death row inmates and was where Federal death sentences were carried out. Fareed's lawyers wanted the death penalty. There are no women here—well, no females, although some take on that role.

ADX philosophy was to try to take violent career prisoners and reform them over a period of 6 security levels. Fareed would never see the outside world again. He would never know that what he had been searching for was literally right in front of him the whole time.

I informed Freddy that I wouldn't be going on any overseas missions in the near future. Abdul had been contained and we were waiting out his next moves. Although I knew Freddy always had a soft spot for me, it was amplified by his conscious, as he'd introduced me to Fareed. He was guilt-ridden over the injuries I'd sustained and the time away from my family. I tried to console him that he was the best in the field, and there was no evidence to indicate there were two people, both messed-up psychopaths.

By March, we were still thigh-deep in snow in Montana, but the glorious sun made it feel much warmer than what it was. The kids were about to get off a week for spring break and we were trying to figure out what last minute trip to take. I was thinking a beach with tropical drinks. The kids had a few friends over, playing pool and eating pizza, when I got a call from Freddy.

"You sitting down for this?" he said in a solemn tone.

"Shoot."

"We lost Abdul. He slipped our surveillance teams somehow and skipped out of the country. Want to take a guess where we think he is heading?"

"WTF, Freddy? Let me see, I get three guesses and only one counts, right? Hmmm. I'll say Russia."

"It seems that our old friend Ivan Karpov was just the tip of this. They have been colluding with the Russians, and infiltrated social media platforms to rig the Presidential election. You know what this means, don't you?"

"Yep, I sure do. I need to go. I'll get back to you."

Tom came up with a bottle of Chateau Montelana Estate Cabernet and grabbed us a glass from the bar. I looked at the kids clowning around and made a mental note to help them with their trick shots when their friends left. It called to mind that they'd be leaving for college next fall and Tom and I would be alone for the first time since we met. School shootings in the U.S. were a common occurrence now, with daily frequency. We were sending our kids out into this mad, mad world.

I looked at Tom and said, "I have something I need to tell you." He could tell by the look in my eyes it was something significant.

"Oh, no. Can it at least wait until the kids leave for the movies?" he said dryly but almost pleading.

"Sure."

The kids were all laughing, having fun. Their friends were nice and made cordial conversation with parents, something you don't see much of these days, with this generation. One of them asked me what I did for a living and I explained how I was tenured as a flight attendant and got to travel the world; that's why he probably didn't see me when we first moved here. My kids were all laughing, telling their friends not to listen to me, explaining to them not to listen to what I say, as I exaggerated everything, and I was the true AESOP fable-teller.

I laughed and took another sip of wine...If only they knew.

I lean back and listen to *Feeling Good* by Muse
...It's a new dawn...It's a new day...And I'm feeling good...

About the Author

This is a FICTIONAL book with some very minute elements of truth from my life. No, not the guns and military stuff (you idiot, I took most of that off Google). I just said it's a FICTIONAL book. I'm not that smart, really; I just wrote about whatever I heard on TV or the radio on any given day.

My husband does watch *The Bachelor* (and of course, The Bachelorette), and I have 3 kids, but they are not triplets. I do have two dogs; they are fat labs.

I habitually watch any movie with Keanu Reeves, Kurt Russell, Mel Gibson, Tom Cruise or Bruce Willis. I also watch *Jaws, The Notebook,* and *The Holiday* every time it's on.

I prefer 70s music. I cannot for the life of me tell you the name of artists or titles of any songs despite singing it thousand times, with the exception of Tom Petty and Barbara Streisand.

What can I say? I have issues.

I wonder who will play me in the movie? Jennifer Lawrence would be awesome. Wait, Blake Lively would be great! #BringRyan!! Reese Witherspoon is probably too sweet to play this type role. Jennifer Garner would be good and probably closer to my age (actually, closer to my husband's age) ... And how about Queen B for Bethany?!

Please stop now and go catch up on real news and go educate yourself...for the love of God.

"You're still here? It's over. Go home. Go."

"Leave the Gun. Take the Cannolis."

Ok, really? Why are you still reading? Go get help.

Excerpt from the upcoming *Another Aesop*

"What madness is it to be expecting evil before it comes."
– Lucius Seneca

China has more cameras than anyone in the world—over 600 million. Facial recognition software is allowing the country to create their own cast system to support the communist party. If your child says something against the party, it affects ALL family members. It changes how you get loans, jobs, what you can buy, and who you hang out with. You can't get out of it.

Reminds me of Tom Cruise in *Minority Report*. Is it life imitating art, or is art imitating life? Doesn't matter, it has a global consequence that we can't allow. After all, it is a mad, mad world.

Barracuda by Heart...*So this ain't the end... I saw you again today...I bet you gonna ambush me...*

Follow for more information and insights:
Instagram: @aesopstories

First Printing, July 2018

Made in the USA
Lexington, KY
11 November 2018